And then he saw her...

And everything inside him stopped to focus, personal and professional attention completely engaged.

She stood at the top of the steps, her auburn hair burnished to molten copper by the sun. Deep waves cupped her temples, flaring out at her cheekbones, then dipping in again at her chin as though Jose Eber himself had prepared her for a Rapunzel Hair Products thirty-second spot.

For a moment Brandon couldn't speak. She was perfect. Or at least she appeared to be. But was her hair long enough for the fairy-tale effect he had planned?

Then, as though this were indeed a magical place where everything came out right, a midmorning wind blew off the lake, making a sudden dark-fire explosion of the redhead's hair.

It swirled above her, floated across her face, flew out to the side like a banner of claret silk. Then the wind moved on and she raised a hand to toss her hair back.

Brandon's heart picked up its beat as her fingers threaded through a good eighteen inches of hair. This couldn't be real!

He closed his eyes to test his senses, and when he opened them, she was gone....

Dear Reader,

Once upon a time we were little girls dreaming of handsome princes on white chargers, of fairy godmothers who'd made us into beautiful princesses, and of mountain castles where we'd live happily ever after.

Now that we're all grown up, we can recapture those dreams in a brand-new miniseries, ONCE UPON A KISS. It features stories based on some of the world's best-loved fairy tales—expressly for the little girl who still lives on inside of us.

Muriel Jensen leads off the series with the retelling of the romantic Rapunzel and her dashing prince who scaled the tower to win his lady love.

Be sure to read all six of these wonderful fairy-tale romances, coming to you every other month, only from American Romance!

ONCE UPON A KISS—at the heart of every little girl's dreams...and every woman's fantasy....

Happy reading!

Debra Matteucci
Senior Editor & Editorial Coordinator
Harlequin Books
300 East 42nd Street
New York, NY 10017

Muriel Jensen

THE PRINCE, THE LADY & THE TOWER

Harlequin Books

TORONTO • NEW YORK • LONDON
AMSTERDAM • PARIS • SYDNEY • HAMBURG
STOCKHOLM • ATHENS • TOKYO • MILAN
MADRID • WARSAW • BUDAPEST • AUCKLAND

To Ron...my prince

ISBN 0-373-16669-9

THE PRINCE, THE LADY & THE TOWER

Prologue

Once upon a time there lived a handsome Prinz named Brandon, who was vice president in charge of marketing for the king of Rampion Pharmaceuticals. He lived in a castle surrounded by a beautiful garden in a land called California.

Sometimes he was happy, but sometimes he would wander into the garden at night and look up at the stars and know that there was much missing in his life that he could never have.

At the northern tip of the kingdom, there lived a very beautiful woman with long, glorious hair that flamed like the maple leaf in October. She had a shop in the village on a high mountain, and lived with a witch at the edge of the forest.

Sometimes she was happy, but sometimes she would wander into the forest and listen to the birds and wish for a prince to ride out of the trees, sweep her up onto his horse, and take her to his castle where there was laughter and dancing.

Chapter One

"Gentlemen, we need drastic action. The Rampion hair-care division has lost money for the past five years. We're not leaving this boardroom until we have a workable plan to prevent that from happening next year. Now, come on. What's our problem? We can sell aspirin, cold remedies, bandages, bath products. Why is the hair-care division failing?"

Bill McCormick, a tall, sandy-haired young man in charge of finance, leaned back in his chair. "Mike, why do we *care* that it's failing?" he asked. "Every other division of Rampion is outselling its competitors. Let's just go with what we know we can do and dump the hair stuff."

Sandra Hudson, seated beside McCormick, folded her arms on the table and nodded reluctantly. "I hate to agree with Bill on anything, but he might be right, Mike. There's too much proliferation of product for anybody to get a good share of the market. I know you have a sentimental attachment to the hair-care division because it was your wife's proj—"

"U.S. consumers spend 4.5 billion a year to groom their hair," Brandon Prinz interrupted, and handed

Sandra a report with a red cover. He walked around the table, distributing more copies of the report. "One point seven billion on shampoo, one billion on conditioners, 600 million on hairspray, 500 million on gels and mousses. I think there's enough to go around that we can claim our share of the market. We did it once. We can do it again. All we have to do is figure out what's wrong with our approach and fix it."

Wade Bennett pushed his water glass aside to open up the report. "Jeez. Look at these comparison figures." He frowned at Brandon through round, wire-rimmed glasses. "You're sure the problem isn't with our product?"

Reports distributed, Brandon went to a box on the console behind him. "Absolutely. Check page three. I've compared our ingredients with theirs and ours are better."

He pulled their product in its packaging out of the box and held it up. "In fact, our lab says we're the best shampoo and conditioner on the market. We've perfected the balance of silicone oil and cleansing agent for a conditioner that actually stays on after the rinse out. We should be number one on drugstore shelves."

He placed a Rampion shampoo and conditioner bottle in front of every board member, then placed a cluster of competitors' products in the middle of the table. "So, why aren't we?"

Sandra reached for two bottles and held them out toward Brandon as he resumed his chair. "Something jumps right out at me. These two products are using

Awapuhi or Tea tree oil, but we don't. Everyone knows they're wonderful for the hair.''

''Why?'' he asked.

She looked momentarily surprised, then she squared her shoulders and cleared her throat. ''Tea tree oil comes from Australia and...um...adds...shine, I think.''

Brandon shook his head and tapped a finger on the report in front of him. ''Check page six.'' He smiled at Sandra's luxurious, though short, blond hair. ''You do have great hair, Sandy, but it isn't thanks to the Tea tree oil in your shampoo.'' He grinned at her. ''We'll talk later about why you're not using *our* product.''

She stammered an excuse, but her co-workers' teasing laughter drowned it out.

''The Tea tree oil,'' Brandon continued, ''would have benefit as an antibacterial and healing agent if there was enough of it in your shampoo to have an impact and if it wasn't combined with the water pressure from your shower. The truth is, it can't cling to the scalp during rinsing. Advertising made you believe Tea tree oil was doing something for your hair that it can't do.''

She skimmed the page he indicated, then looked up at him in distress. ''But Awapuhi...''

''Is an extract of a Hawaiian ginger plant, but there's no evidence it does anything for scalp or hair, particularly in the minute amounts you find in a bottle of shampoo.''

''So, you're saying all these manufacturers are lying?'' McCormick asked.

Brandon grinned. "I think they'd say they were taking creative liberties with the truth."

Wade leaned eagerly toward Brandon. "Can't we do that?"

Mike Rampion, president and chairman of the board, shook his head. "Never. We've never lied to our customers. We don't use animal testing, we don't pollute and we donate ten percent of profits to green causes. We're going to bring Rampion Hair Care Products back another way." He turned to Brandon with a vaguely concerned expression. "But how?"

"A completely new approach," Brandon replied. "We need a more impressive look." He held up their very ordinary, round plastic bottle. "We can sell the benefits of our product to the consumer without lies and with new packaging, a new name, a new slogan."

McCormick rolled his eyes. "That's a lot of money to invest in the same place we've lost money before. And we'll need an ad agency…"

"No, we won't." Brandon turned to a dark-haired young woman seated beside him, who appeared to be doing her best to remain unnoticed. When he directed his attention to her, she seemed to shrink away. "You all know Betsy Shaffer, Rampion's own little self-contained art and graphics department."

Everyone around the table nodded and smiled at her, but skeptically. There was a murmur of greetings.

"Hi," she said in a near whisper, peering around Brandon.

"Betsy and I have been brainstorming for a couple of days," he said, encouraging her to her feet as he spoke, "and she has a brilliant idea."

"Well, the tower thing was your..." she began to correct quietly.

"Tell them," he said, taking her arm and gently turning her away from him toward the board members gathered around the table.

She tugged at the hem of a navy blue jacket that matched her skirt. "We...thought...we should go with a fairy-tale approach."

There was an immediate murmur of disapproval. The men looked at one another doubtfully and Sandra asked in a flat tone, "Fairy tale? As in *Cinderella?*"

Sandra stood a little straighter. "No. As in *Rapunzel*. We thought...we'd change the name to Rapunzel Hair Products, highlight all the real benefits to a woman's hair rather than all the fibs everybody else is telling, mold our bottle to look like a stone tower, just like in the fairy tale, and make our tag line..." She turned to Brandon. "Mr. Prinz should tell you that part, because the slogan was his idea." She sat down.

"Wait a minute." Sandra looked around the table for the corroboration of her co-workers disapproval. She had it. "You can't sell today's woman with a *fairy tale*. She's savvy, hardworking, analytical. She—"

"I know," Brandon interrupted. "She's the first woman in the history of the world to hold so many jobs, to make so much money, to make so many contributions to her world. So, in the privacy of her home life—and in the intimacy of her bedroom..." He smiled around the table. "Why can't she have fairy-tale hair?"

Every man in the room leaned back in his chair, concentrating on the image. Betsy turned to Brandon with a shy smile. He winked at her. Sandra, who sported a time-efficient short bob, rolled her eyes in disgust.

"I think it'll sell," Betsy said in a quiet voice directed at Mike Rampion, "because Brandon's right. Women have to be controlled and practical in every other phase of their lives, so it stands to reason they'll jump at a product that promises that wonderful fairy-tale hair you see in Mucha posters and...here." She held up the middle pages of a large-format child's book of the *Rapunzel* fairy tale. A lavish illustration of the heroine, her glorious blond hair billowing about her, crossed both pages. "And without lies, we can give her the best hair-care products on the market— and she'll buy them because our promotion and packaging will be too inviting to resist."

Mike slapped a hand atop the report before him. "Damned if you aren't brilliant, Betsy."

She beamed. "Well, a lot of the ideas were Brandon's."

Mike turned to the man whose marketing strategies had doubled Rampion Pharmaceuticals' sales in the past five years. "What's the slogan?"

Brandon smiled and spread both hands as though the idea were so simple he was reluctant to take credit for it. "Let your hair down with Rapunzel Hair Products."

There was laughter, then applause that grew louder as the beautiful simplicity of the idea came home to everyone.

"We need a spokeswoman," Brandon said when

the room was quiet again. "One woman for print and television advertising."

"A celebrity?" Sandra asked.

"Betsy thought an unknown would be a better choice," he replied. "Someone the average woman could relate to better than she could to a Hollywood face."

"Isn't Hollywood fairy tale enough?"

Brandon ignored the sarcasm in Sandra's question. "No. Hollywood is fantasy, but not necessarily fairy tale. We want to pitch the nice-heroine image. Show them your storyboards, Betsy."

Betsy spread out her proposed campaign across the table, and everyone leaned over it with enthusiasm. By midafternoon, she had everyone's support and creative contributions, even Sandra's.

By dinnertime, Mike Rampion was convinced that they were about to make a major marketing coup. He praised them all for their assistance, promised Betsy a raise and kept Brandon in his office after everyone else had gone home.

"Thank you." Mike opened the gray, raw silk, floor-to-ceiling draperies until the panorama of downtown Los Angeles was spread out before them like a jeweled relief against a black-velvet sky. He turned back to his desk and fell with a small groan into the high-backed black leather chair.

Brandon, his jacket tossed aside and his tie pulled away from his throat, sprawled in the smaller chrome-and-black-leather chair that faced the desk. "For what?" he asked, fingers laced over his stomach. "That's what you pay me for."

"No," Mike corrected. "There isn't enough money to pay for the effort and the wily genius you put into a project. I wanted very much to save this one, and it looks like you're going to make that possible."

Brandon peered into Mike's green eyes. They were tired now from the long and challenging day, but still alive with the wit and intelligence that had made a business grow through the past twenty, difficult years.

Under the shrewd gaze, he could see the kindness and the generosity that had encouraged him to take in an adolescent ruffian and give him the first taste of security he'd known in thirteen years. There was no way in the world to repay that kind of gift, but he kept trying.

"Yeah, well, Ruthie would come back to haunt you if you let the hair-care division go. What're you doing for dinner? Dunston's off tonight."

"Hadn't thought about it. Don't you have plans?"

"Nope. I was thinking Kate Mantilini's sounded good. Then we can go home and watch Leno and drink brandy and figure out where in the hell we're going to find a woman with perfect hair a yard long and a face all America will relate to."

Mike grinned. "If we found a woman like that, I'm not sure I'd want to share her with all of America. You're not spending too much time at home on my account, are you? I've been released from the doctor's care. I'm fine. There's no need for you to hover. If you had plans tonight..."

Brandon pushed himself out of the chair and went to the chrome coatrack in the corner. He tossed Mike's brown herringbone jacket to him and shrugged into his own gray pin-striped one.

"I said I didn't have any plans," he reiterated, "Now, let's get out of here before Mantilini's gets too crowded for us to get a table."

Mike stood and pulled on his coat. "Because while I appreciate you behaving like the son Ruthie and I were never blessed with, I don't want you to ever feel obli—"

"All I'm feeling right now is hungry. Could you speed it up?" Brandon helped him with the left sleeve, then pulled the office door open.

Mike walked to the door, adjusting the cuffs of his shirt below the hem of his jacket sleeves. "Would you listen to me?" he demanded impatiently.

Brandon held the doorknob and leaned his weight on one foot. "How can I help it? You keep going on and on. What? I did *not* have plans for tonight. I am *not* hovering over you. I do *not* feel obligated to you."

Mike looked him in the eye.

Brandon did his best to hold his gaze without betraying that the last denial, at least, was untrue. He felt obligated to Mike for his very life.

"Dr. Hunniger told me that if I'm careful and heed that warning, my heart will outlast the rest of me."

"Good." Brandon made a sweeping motion through the door, trying to encourage Mike to move on. "Because my stomach's about to give up on both of us."

But Mike stood resolutely in place, his expression firm. There'd been a time in Brandon's life when that look would have sent him into immediate repentance and, on occasion, into hiding.

"I gave you a home," Mike said, his voice quiet with sincerity, "because you were the most resourceful, reliable and courageous kid I'd ever seen, and we both happened to find ourselves without family at the same time. And we've done well together. But there's no way I'm going to let you live your life for me out of some misbegotten sense of duty."

Brandon resigned himself to having to settle the issue once and for all. "I may have been misbegotten, but my sense of duty springs from a deep and abiding love for and gratitude to you, and no amount of ultimatums on your part is going to change that. But duty isn't keeping me home tonight—an empty calendar is. And since I've always found you to be an interesting dinner companion, I thought we could eat together. But if you're going to get all maudlin and psychological on me, I'll just…"

Mike shook his head at him and walked through the open doorway. "Oh, shut up and let's go."

"Right."

ANGIE CORWIN PUT the finishing touches on a white-chocolate-and-raspberry *gâteau* and took a step back to admire her handiwork. She sighed with satisfaction. It was more than handiwork; it was artwork. She was the Degas of desserts, the Gauguin of *gâteaux*. The raspberry top was crisscrossed with latticework icing dotted where the lines connected with silver dragées. In the center was a white-chocolate rose.

Angie pulled off her apron and sighed with satisfaction. She looked around at the well-appointed and well stocked little kitchen and decided that even though this was 180 degrees away from where she'd expected to find herself when she graduated from culinary school, she liked it.

It wasn't the five-star, cosmopolitan hotel kitchen where she'd spent the past four years as a sous-chef and cultivated a taste for the insane bustle of the hot spot dinnertime. But it was her own place, with everything where *she* wanted it and a menu *she'd* planned. And after a childhood of being moved from one remote place to another, a young adulthood of longing for the kinds of families other boardinghouse students had and then four years of loving the ambience of a hotel kitchen, but hating the anonymity into which she disappeared when she left it—a little tea shop on the edge of nowhere and her very own mother in her very own country cottage were a happy turn of events for which she was very grateful.

She would be even more grateful, she thought with a grin as she tossed her apron into a laundry bag in the corner, if she could get her mother to cheer up.

An energetic fifty-year-old woman, banished from her lifelong passion for fieldwork in archaeology by painful arthritis, was not amusing company. But Angie had waited years to be able to spend time with her mother, and though she certainly wouldn't have wished this problem on her, she was determined to take advantage of the position in which it placed her— that of being dependent upon her daughter.

The swinging door between the kitchen and the tea shop was pushed in and a dark head peered around it to announce in an excited whisper, "We just sold the *entire* chocolate cherry tart and half the white-chocolate Grand Marnier cheesecake for the school-board meeting tonight, and Mrs. Evans picked up her coffee-and-chestnut pâté. I'll bet she tries to pass it off as her own."

"No problem," Angie whispered back as she made her way toward Becky Flynn. "I'll be putting it on the menu next month, so everyone will know she got it here. Why are we whispering?" Angie stood on tip-toe to see over Becky's head into the tearoom. Which wasn't difficult. Becky barely topped five feet, but what she lacked in height, she made up for in enthu-siasm.

Her husband was a trucker, and in the month since Angie had opened the shop and hired her, she'd come in early and stayed late, willing to give every spare moment her husband was on the road to the unique treat of tea served in fine china on lace tablecloths in the nether reaches of northern California.

"Just a couple of customers dawdling over their muffins and lemon curd," Becky said under her breath. "Also, I wanted to warn you that your mom's on her way." Becky's perpetual smile turned to an uncharacteristic frown. "She's not coming to help, is she?"

Angie had to laugh. Bored with all Angie's efforts to keep her entertained at home, Gretta had come into town several times to "help" at the shop. At a com-plete loss in the kitchen, Gretta relegated her efforts to straightening up the stockroom. But even at that, she was accustomed to running a field team and tended to think of Becky as her employee. And while Becky was willing to extend herself in any direction for Angie, she resented being told what to do by anyone else.

"No," she reassured her quickly. "We're going to dinner and a movie."

Becky breathed a sigh of relief. "Please don't be offended. I love working for you, but your mother makes Napoleon look unassuming. Excuse me. Better check on the ladies."

Angie met her mother in front of the shop. It was early September and the afternoon sun was still warm and golden. "Hi. Did you decide where we should go?"

Gretta was several inches shorter than Angie, the auburn hair she'd bequeathed to her daughter now generously laced with gray and pulled into a loose knot at the back of her head, the same way she'd always worn it in the field.

She wore the designer jeans and a roll-necked white sweater Angie had bought her in an attempt to upscale the cotton pants and T-shirts she'd also always worn in the field and now put on for every occasion.

Gretta sighed. "Well, I miss kabobs and couscous, but since I'm not likely to find them here, I suppose we should opt for the Chinese place."

"Maybe you should open a kabobs-and-couscous place here," Angie suggested as they began the two-block trek to Wah Mae's. "It could be the trend of the late nineties. You could make your fortune."

Gretta cast her a "yeah, right" glance. "The only way I'm going to make my fortune, now that I'm an invalid dependent upon my daughter for a roof over my head, is if I win the lottery. Incidentally—'' She stopped in her tracks and sighed.

Angie braced herself. She knew this look. A confession was imminent.

''I may have broken the teeny record-player thing.''

Her mother was not coping well with new technology. Angie didn't have the VCR back from the shop yet. She smiled patiently. ''It's okay. But they're not teeny records, Mom. They're CDs.''

''They're round.''

Angie dismissed that detail. ''What happened?''

''Well, I couldn't get it to go on, then it came on too loudly and I couldn't find the button to turn it down, and I sort of...punched them all at once.''

Angie looked down at her mother's hands, misshapen from the arthritis, and wondered how she'd done it.

Gretta read her mind. ''I was holding a book at the time.''

Angie dismissed concern over her CD player—it had been bottom-of-the-line anyway—and took pleasure in the fact that her mother had been using her time constructively.

''What were you reading?'' she asked, hooking an arm in her mother's to resume their walk to dinner.

''Nothing,'' Gretta replied. ''I was using the book to press some old photos I found of the Masai and Supuma women I got to know back ho—'' She stopped and corrected herself. ''At the gorge.''

Angie groaned but kept walking. ''Mom,'' she said plaintively, ''you've got to accept your life the way it is now—and you've got to put some effort into it. All this difficulty you're having with household appliances and modern technology is just a manifestation of your frustration at having your life turned around.''

Gretta frowned at her as they stopped at Gray Goose Lake's one and only traffic signal. ''Thank you, Angelyn Jung. Or is it Freud?''

Angie frowned back. ''It's Corwin, Mother, just like you. Just like Daddy. I'm sorry your arthritis cut your career short, but you can still lead a full and useful and even exciting life, if you'll just let go of where you wish you were and accept where you are.''

An emotion Angie couldn't identify passed across her mother's eyes.

''I've always found it so fascinating the way you say that,'' Gretta said.

''What?''

'''Daddy.' As though you really knew him.''

Angie shrugged. She'd always felt as though she had. ''Maybe I did on some level,'' she said, hooking her arm in Gretta's again as the light turned to Walk. ''I might have some genetic memory of him. Or maybe it's just what you've told me about him that made him seem so real.''

''I hate being dependent upon you.''

Gretta had redirected the conversation. Angie had known she would. She always did when the subject of Angie's father came up. Grief, she guessed, had lingered all this time.

''Mom, I'm so happy to be able to spend time with you,'' Angie said earnestly. ''When I got to travel with you when I was little, you were always working and preoccupied with your discoveries, and we've spent so much of the rest of the time apart. I'm thrilled that we're sharing a place."

"Even though I break everything?"

"You'll get over that once you adjust."

"I won't get over the fact that you had to turn your life upside down to accommodate mine. And that you were willing to come here where I was so happy as a girl." They'd reached Wah Mae's and Gretta stopped in the doorway to face Angie, her expression uncharacteristically conciliatory. "You do understand that I'd have never made it in the big city. I'm too used to fresh air, clear skies, trees, rivers…silence."

Angie nodded, trying to make her acceptance clear without making too much of it. Her mother had deep feelings but had difficulty sharing what she felt—and hated a fuss being made of it when she did.

"Of course I do." She looked around herself at the neat little town with its turn-of-the-century architecture that was half Italianate, half cowboy, tucked into lush, wooded hills halfway between Sacramento and the Oregon border. Gray Goose Lake was set against a sky as blue as the Mediterranean, and Angie had difficulty finding fault with it. "This is a beautiful spot. We'll be happy here."

Gretta looked into her eyes, trying to read the truth. Angie put on her best honest, innocent smile. That was one of the few assets of having freckles—they made it easier to look honest and innocent.

Apparently satisfied, her mother shook a crooked index finger at Angie. "I'm going to find a way to earn money to pay my own way. You'll see."

Angie rolled her eyes. "Mom, we've been over this."

"Well, then, we'll go over it again. I was looking through my diaries that were in the same box with the photographs, and I was thinking I might be able to put together a book."

Angie stopped protesting. "That's a wonderful idea. You can put all your thoughts on tape, and I'll type it up for you."

"Angie, you don't have a spare minute to call your own as it is."

"Then you can do it after we have that surgery on your hands."

Angie discovered that those misshapen hands could still be used to shake her. "Forget the surgery! You are not going to spend your hard-earned money…"

Angie took hold of her mother's arms and did her own shaking. "Do not tell me what to do. I told you when we decided to move in together that we're going to be equal partners. You're not going to push me around like some flunkie on your dig."

"'Equal' being the operative word." Gretta dropped her hands, but not her determined gaze. "That doesn't mean you get to pay for everything my insurance refuses to pick up. I said no to that surgery the first time you brought it up, and I'm saying no to it again. And there are no flunkies on a dig."

"My mistake. But if you're so concerned about paying your own way, I think you'll be more able to do it with hands that *work*."

Gretta considered the logic of that, then drew an

exasperated sigh. "Some day I'm going to *hire* a hand to double into a fist and punch you in the nose."

Angie pulled the restaurant door open. "Nice loving words, Mother. You're sitting alone at the movies."

"Oh, lighten up. Somebody has to unwrap my candy bar for me."

Chapter Two

"I like the brunette," Wade Bennett said. "And her hair's longer than the blonde's." He pulled the model's photo out of the lineup of five in the middle of the boardroom table.

"Nice hair but hard face," McCormick said, reaching for another one of the photos. "What about this blonde? I mean, if we're going for fairy tales, aren't all princesses blond?"

"Snow White wasn't," Sandra said. "She was brunette. I like this one." In deference to her continued insistence on a model more appropriate to the working-girl image, Mike had included one with chin-length hair when they'd narrowed the photos down to five. That was the photo she held up.

"No," Bennett insisted. "Short hair doesn't sell shampoo."

"Then we'll get her a hair weave."

Mike shook his head. "You're missing the point, Sandy. We want this to be real and honest."

Sandra pointed to the photo before her. "Short hair is today's woman's reality. It's easier to take care of and takes less time. And if you insist on being real, why are we trying to sell her a fairy tale?''

''Because *we* have to be honest,'' Brandon said. ''But our customer is entitled to fairy-tale hair.''

''Who's your choice?'' Bennett asked Brandon.

Brandon glanced at the two photos left, one of a long, loosely permed dark blonde and the other a strawberry blonde with a Gibson-girl knot, and shook his head. ''Pretty faces and pretty hair, but none of them really has...the right look.''

Sandra frowned at him. ''You might be looking for some perfect ideal that doesn't exist...except in a fairy tale.''

Brandon nodded. ''That's exactly the point. She has to look like she just walked out of *Rapunzel*.''

''All right.'' Mike stood. ''Let's put that aside for a while. You all have your jobs to do to push the project ahead. We'll just give the model issue a rest for the time being.''

''But if you want to have this on the market anytime soon...'' McCormick began worriedly.

Mike nodded and silenced him with a raised hand. ''I know. We have to make a decision. Leave it to me.''

The group filed out, eager to be relieved of the responsibility on a sunny Friday afternoon. When they'd left, Mike gathered up the photos and dropped them back into the envelope containing all the photos from which they'd narrowed the decision.

Brandon stood and stretched. ''I thought you didn't like any of them, either.''

Mike stood resolutely and yanked his jacket off the back of his chair. "I don't. We're starting fresh."

"You mean...new models?"

"I'm not sure what I mean. But we need a fresh outlook. You have plans for the next week?"

Brandon thought a moment. "Nothing that can't wait." Then he understood what Mike had in mind. "We're gathering up notes and photos and taking them to the lake, where everything always goes right for you. Am I *right?*"

"Yes. Does that work for you? I know you tend to get bored up there, but we should be able to get this together in a week, tops."

He wanted to groan, but instead he nodded. "Sure. Works fine."

BRANDON PACKED a bag, the fishing pole Mike had given him two birthdays ago, a couple of CDs, a novel and his laptop and stowed them in the trunk of Mike's silver blue Lexus. It wasn't that he didn't like the lake, but as a child of the streets, he'd grown up surrounded by asphalt and brick and continuous activity. In the heart of a big city, a child left alone to fend for himself didn't have to starve. There were options—soup kitchens, the dumpsters of dozens of restaurants, produce vendors who'd take pity on a kid and give him a banana in exchange for an errand run.

Brandon had been about fourteen the first time Mike had taken him to the lake, and he'd almost panicked. There was nothing but the incredible blue of the water, the vastness of a clear sky, a forest that was beautiful but spooky, with nothing in it that he could identify as edible, and a dinky little five-block town.

He'd come close to hyperventilating. Though Mike had taken him in a year earlier, he hadn't allowed himself to settle in. He'd done his chores, kept his room clean and held down a part-time job at a supermarket to make sure he had a little cash when someone from Children's Services came along and made him move again.

They'd been fishing in the little Bayliner Mike had rented for the month of August. Mike had adjusted the brim of his baseball cap and said casually, "Fishing's supposed to be fun, you know. Relax your grip on the pole. If we don't catch anything, we've got kitchen cupboards filled with food, or there's even a couple of restaurants where we can get something to eat."

Brandon had been embarrassed. "Sorry," he'd said, trying to loosen the muscles in his arms and shoulders. When his father had been drunk for days and Brandon hadn't wanted to be there when he woke up, food had become a priority for him—and in his vigilant young mind, the fact that he was fishing for it instead of foraging in a dumpster, didn't change that.

"You're my foster son now, Brandon," Mike had said. "You don't have to worry about fending for yourself anymore. I'll take care of you. I promised you that when you moved in."

"I know," he'd replied. "I trust you. But somebody'll come along and make me move. Happens all the time. I've got to keep my skills up."

Mike had laughed, told him not to borrow trouble and said he had the makings of a businessman. "You work hard, and even when you decide to trust some-one, you never let your guard down. Those are good qualities in the marketplace, but man to man..." He'd pointed to himself, then tapped a finger against Brandon's heart. "Friendships require different things from you. You got to relax, trust, leave your gut vulnerable."

He'd understood the advice; he'd just never been entirely able to implement it—except with Mike.

So, for the sake of the man who'd made life livable, and in the interest of the plan to save the hair-care products division, he could put up with a week in the boonies. He'd been to Gray Goose Lake at least once a year since then, and now knew that the kitchen cupboards in Mike's converted barn were filled with canned goods, that the freezer was well stocked and that he was a good enough hand with a rod and reel to catch a fish if it was out there. And if all else failed, he had considerable cash, gold cards of every variety and the little Chinese place made the best kung pao on the West Coast. He had nothing to fear.

But it was curious, he thought, as he slammed the trunk closed, walked around to the driver's side and climbed in beside Mike, that once you were forced to admit fear, it lost its teeth—but you still knew it was out there and perfectly capable of gumming you to death, if you let it.

"MAYBE WE NEED to look at faces from another agency." Mike was pacing the floor, which was scattered with brightly colored rugs in the vaulted-ceilinged living room. Comfortable mission furniture in red and green formed a U in the middle of the vast space, and a little fire in the fieldstone fireplace took the chill off the early-September morning.

The portfolio photos were strewn all over the dining table, the coffee table and every other flat surface that would accommodate them.

Brandon, foraging in the kitchen, turned away from the refrigerator to reply, "We've got faces from *every* agency. We've already got the modeling world thinking we're perverts. Maybe the woman we're imagining doesn't exist. Cheese? Apple?"

"No."

"No apple or no cheese?"

"No, your instincts are usually right on the money. This woman does exist—she just isn't a model. Get your face out of the fridge. We're going for a walk."

"Come on, Mike," Brandon implored, "I did thirty minutes on the NordicTrack before breakfast."

Mike pulled on an off-white cardigan with leather elbow patches. "We need fresh air."

"I'll open a window."

"Are you coming, or are you fired?"

Brandon slammed the refrigerator door closed and grumbled as he followed Mike to the back door. "You know, you're going to mar me psychologically by switching from father-figure to employer. It might affect my ability to market your products."

"Better not." Mike pushed out onto the broad back deck that looked out onto the lake. Geese swam lazily on the sun-dappled water rimmed with little cottages and rickety-looking docks. "It might affect your inheritance."

"I thought you disinherited me when I went to Stanford instead of Cal."

"Fortunately for you, my attorney went to Stanford and refused to change my will. Okay, now, pay attention. Look for a beautiful woman. And don't stop me every five minutes to ask me if we can break for coffee. This is a business expedition."

"Somebody forget his prunes this morning?"

"Shut up and walk."

They set off side by side up a paved road, then stopped when they reached the sidewalk and the carved wooden sign welcoming visitors to Gray Goose Lake, population 1,312.

The morning sun glinted off shop windows and automobiles and gleamed on the star-shaped leaves of the liquidambar planted at intervals on both sides of the street.

The air was perfumed with fall—the lingering scent of flowers, the pungent woodsmoke coming from the homes several blocks over and the indefinable bite of the changing season. Shouts and laughter came from the direction of the grade school on a back street. Recess.

Brandon drew a breath of the intoxicating air and felt it clear his head, sharpen his senses. The past few days of trying to force the right face out of the photos he knew to be wrong had been mind-numbing. But he had doubts about this approach working.

"You really think we're going to pass the right face walking down the street in Gray Goose Lake?"

"Of course not, but maybe we'll see a face that'll spark an idea or give us a clue to what we want."

Brandon and Mike walked slowly up Lakefront Drive, pretending to take in the town's comfortable ambience while subtly watching faces. They were greeted by the owner of the shoe store, who was outside sweeping the sidewalk and recognized them as part-time residents, and by the manager of an appliance store, who'd sold them a microwave, a television and a VCR over the years.

A woman emerged from a flower shop, pushing a display cart filled with colorful mums, bunches of eucalyptus and dried flowers. She placed the cart in front of the shop's window and smiled at them before going back inside. She had shoulder-length dark hair and was very pretty, but was somewhere in her forties.

A young woman walked by pushing a two-seated stroller. She had blond hair bunched into a ponytail and was also quite pretty, but bore the look of bone weariness worn by mothers of very young children.

They passed older women in sweats on power walks, a pretty young woman with a buzz cut, a beautiful black woman with dreadlocks.

At the opposite end of the downtown area, Brandon grinned at Mike as they crossed the street. "Sure you don't want to go for coffee?" he asked.

"Yes, I'm sure," Mike replied, then smiled at a pair of older ladies carrying grocery bags. "Now, concentrate. There's an answer here somewhere. I know it."

Brandon did his best to cooperate. He wandered beside Mike down the other side of Lakefront Drive. Mike pulled him to a stop, pointing to a young woman with long, dark hair looking in the window of a pet shop.

Then a young man from several doors up called to her, and she turned to reveal pretty blue eyes, a bright smile with perfect teeth and a pretty little nose—with a ring in it.

"My God," Mike groaned mournfully under his breath. "Why do women do that?"

Brandon shrugged. "Got me. Personal expression, I guess. Come on. There's a beauty shop up ahead. We'll hide out in the computer shop next door and watch for pretty heads."

"You just want to lust after the stuff in the tearoom window across the street."

"Right. Like you'd catch me in a tea shop."

Mike and Brandon pretended to pore over a display of graphics software in the window of Lakefront Laptops. Through it they could see women coming and going from Cindy's Hair Fair.

After almost half an hour, Mike sighed dispiritedly. "We've seen big hair, gray hair, permed hair, peroxided hair and hardly there hair. Could I have been wrong?"

"Before I answer that, am I in the will now or out? I forget."

"Out. So just be honest."

Brandon laughed lightly. "You're not wrong. I think you just attach more magic to this place than any little town can be held accountable for. I know you fell in love here as a young man. I know you've always solved your problems here. But this one involves another human being—and a woman at that. You might just be asking too much of even the most benevolent..."

And then he saw her. *Her!* And everything inside him stopped to focus, personal and professional attention completely engaged.

She was stopped at the top of the post-office steps, a young woman of average height and better-than-average figure in a blue denim jumper over a crisp white shirt. She wore black stockings and black, flat-soled shoes and appeared to be engrossed in an armload of mail—catalogs, he guessed, judging by their size.

She had auburn hair burnished to molten copper by the sun. Wispy bangs. Parted in the middle with deep waves cupping her temples, flaring out at her cheekbones, then dipping in again at her chin, as though José Eber himself had prepared her for a Rapunzel Hair Products thirty-second spot.

For a moment, Brandon couldn't speak. She was perfect. Or at least she appeared to be. But was her hair long enough for the fairy-tale effect he and Betsy had planned?

Then, as though this were indeed a magic place where everything came out right, a midmorning wind blew off the lake, swept up Lakefront Drive, flapping storefront awnings and decorative windsocks—and making a sudden dark-fire explosion of the redhead's hair.

It swirled above her, floated across her face, flew out to the side like a banner of claret silk. Then the wind moved on and she raised a hand to toss her hair back and finger-comb it into place.

Brandon's heart picked up its beat as her fingers

threaded through a good eighteen inches of hair. It had to reach the middle of her back. This couldn't be real.

He closed his eyes to test his senses, and when he opened them again, she was gone. But not far. She was walking up the street, the mail tucked in a big natural-leather drawstring backpack slung over her shoulder.

Brandon backhanded Mike's arm.

"What?" Mike demanded.

Brandon pointed subtly in the redhead's direction.

"My God!" Mike breathed. "Will you look at that *hair!*"

"She's perfect." Brandon spoke absently, his attention on the unconsciously graceful way she moved and the delicacy of her profile—all he could see from across the street.

"We have to see her face," Mike said. "Up close."

As he said the words, she turned into the Tintagel Tearoom. Her hair *did* reach the middle of her back.

Mike turned to him with a teasing grin.

Brandon ran a hand down his face, drew a breath and said flatly, "Like I said, I really want to visit a tearoom."

The inside of the Tintagel confirmed Brandon's worst fears about such a place. A dozen small, round tables were scattered over a moss-green carpet and covered with lace tablecloths. Spindly chairs were pulled up to them, and in the middle of every table was a fat, round pink teapot. China cups and saucers and dessert plates were at every place.

Across the room was a vast glass showcase on a mahogany buffet that displayed a myriad of sinfully rich-looking desserts. Beside it was what appeared to be a refrigerated case with sliced meats and cheeses, pâtés and various fruit and vegetable plates.

Brandon was horrified when Mike moved to a table and pulled out a chair. Four of the other tables were occupied by clusters of women who looked up at them with puzzled interest.

Brandon considered the spindly chair as a receptacle for his six foot two, 184 pounds and dismissed it. But Mike sat and glowered up at him.

"Sit down," he said genially, though his eyes threatened mayhem if Brandon didn't comply. "You've been wanting coffee all morning."

When Mike's weight didn't splinter the chair and send him crashing to the carpet in a heap, Brandon eased himself into the chair opposite, still not entirely sure he wouldn't end up on the floor.

The chair held.

That problem solved, he scanned the room, looking for the redhead. She wasn't there.

Mike frowned at him after his own scan of the area. "Maybe she went into the kitchen. She might work here."

That sounded reasonable.

A petite, dark-haired young woman in a turn-of-the-century frilly white ruffled apron over a high-collared blouse and long skirt approached their table with a decidedly late-twentieth-century smile.

"Good morning, gentlemen," she said. "I would guess you're interested in Irish breakfast tea, Caravan, or black coffee."

Brandon felt instant relief. "Coffee, please."

Mike glanced doubtfully toward the case of elegant desserts. "Would you have an apple Danish among all those beautiful treats?"

"No. Sorry. But we do have a delicious tea brack. Lots of raisins and spices..." she winked "...and half a cup of Irish whiskey goes into the batter."

Mike looked at Brandon for a decision.

Brandon laughed. "How could anything with half a cup of whiskey be bad? Make it two, please."

"And, miss?" Mike raised a hand for her attention as she turned away to fill their orders.

She turned back, a questioning smile in place.

"We noticed a pretty redhead come in here just a minute ago." He looked around again as though to reassure himself she wasn't visible. "Did you see her?"

The waitress nodded. "Yes. That's the boss." The slightest edge of suspicion came into her manner. "Why?"

"I...ah...know her father, but I've lost touch over the past few years. I thought...she could tell me how to reach him."

Brandon closed his eyes, certain that sounded as lame to the waitress as it sounded to him.

When he opened them again, it was just in time to see her give Mike, and then him, a very distrustful look. Then she smiled politely. "Sorry. You just missed her. This is her day off. If you want to leave your card, I can have her get in touch with you."

Good girl, Brandon thought.

Mike reached instinctively for his breast pocket, then realized he was wearing a sweater. He spread both hands helplessly. "Haven't got one with me," he said, looking embarrassed under the waitress's growing suspicion. "I'll drop one off tomorrow."

She nodded, not entirely hiding her disbelief, and went away to fill their order.

"You lost touch with her *father?*" Brandon said quietly across the table. "That was pathetic!"

Mike quelled him with a look. "So, lying isn't my thing. I didn't hear you say anything to help."

"That's because it took you all of ninety seconds to convince her we're a pair of stalkers. Relax. We've got a name. We'll look her up in the phone book."

The waitress returned with a coffee carafe, filled their tiny cups, then went away with the pink teapot. Brandon wondered if the tiny cups were their punishment for looking suspicious.

"When did we get a name?" Mike asked.

Brandon indicated the long, narrow, painted sign over the doorway into the kitchen. It was done on a scrolled board in the tradition of old inns and taverns.

Tintagel Tearoom, it read. Angelyn Corwin, Prop.

"'Angelyn,'" Mike read aloud. "Pretty name. What's Tintagel?"

"King Arthur's family home."

"I thought that was Camelot."

"Tintagel belonged to Arthur's father," Brandon corrected, but he wasn't thinking about the beauty of her name or the unusual name of the tea shop. The picture of the woman the moment the wind danced with her was forever imprinted on his mind.

ANGELYN CORWIN WAS not in the phone book.

"You think she's new here?" Mike asked.

Brandon closed the book and let it fall to hang from its chain in the phone booth. "Must be. Even if she didn't want her name in the book, she'd want her business to be reachable by phone."

"What do we do now?"

"Wait until tomorrow, and go back to the shop for more tea brack while she's there. Only, I'm bringing my own chair this time."

Mike didn't like that idea. "We don't want to talk to her at work. She'll be pressured and distracted. We have to find out where she lives."

"All right. I'm for that. How?"

"You're the one who lived on the street and claimed to have underworld connections."

"I lied. I wanted to scare you into leaving me alone."

"Well, I'll leave you alone *now* if you don't come up with an idea."

Brandon was trying to concoct a plan, when it suddenly became unnecessary.

Their quarry stepped out of a hardware store half a block up from the phone booth. She carried a hose looped over her shoulder like a lasso, unlocked the door of an old, but tidy burgundy Volvo, stuffed the hose into the back, then climbed in behind the wheel and drove away.

"Then again, maybe we'll just follow her," Brandon said.

"On foot?" Mike demanded.

"She's turning up Mill Road." Brandon craned his neck to watch her progress as a beverage distributor's truck pulled up behind her. "There's nothing up there but a few acreages. We'll go home and get the car, then drive up and look for her car."

The plan worked. The burgundy Volvo was parked in a driveway at the side of a pretty, if dilapidated, white frame cottage that looked as though it belonged on a river in England rather than at the edge of a woods in northern California.

There was an apple tree heavy with fruit in the front yard, from which a slat of wood hung on thick rope for a swing. Around the base of the tree and the front porch of the house were white, gold-centered Shasta daisies.

Brandon pulled the Lexus into the driveway and parked behind the Volvo. He stepped out of the car and was greeted by the sound of country-and-western music coming from an upstairs window.

Mike walked up a narrow, flower-bordered walk that led to the back of the house. Brandon followed and waited while he climbed several steps and knocked on the door.

There was no answer.

On the other side of a deep, broad yard of dry grass stood a small stone building that might be used as a shed or a garage. One of the double doors was open.

Brandon went to the shed, took two steps inside and inhaled a musty smell that was partly earth and partly automotive. Two snow tires lay on a tarpaulin on the concrete floor beside a wheelbarrow filled with lawn clippings.

A flash of movement in the shadows at the back caught his eye and he peered in that direction, trying to distinguish shapes. "Hello?" he called. "Miss Corwin?"

There was an intake of breath, a sudden sharp movement in the shadows to his right, and before he could turn, he felt something curl around his shin and ankle. At the same moment, determined hands caught his arms and tried to knock him off balance and take him down.

In the instant of surprise he experienced before his old street-fighter instincts took over, he realized that although the hands were determined, they weren't very strong.

He pushed back with the skill and swiftness marine corps training added to instinct.

ANGIE KNEW she'd been stupid to try to defend her household herself, but she hadn't known what else to do. She'd seen the two men watching her downtown, then Becky had called with the warning that two men she thought looked shifty had been in the shop looking for her, and when they appeared in her driveway, she'd been desperate. The news was full of crazies assaulting innocent people every day—even in out-of-the-way places like this.

She didn't have a gun, knew she'd never be able to use a knife on anyone, so she'd hidden her mother in the back of the shed with the cordless phone to dial 911 and positioned herself to defend what was hers.

Now, as she flew through the air with some thug's steely arm around her waist, she wished she'd taken that karate class the busgirls at the Tuxedo Junction Restaurant were always trying to talk her into.

She gritted her teeth and screwed her eyes shut, expecting to land on her head on concrete at any moment. But she landed, instead, on a bed of something soft but prickly that rattled with the impact of her weight. The wheelbarrow!

She opened her eyes, now more angry than frightened, and tried to kick at her assailant as he leaned over her to reach for her hands.

But he simply caught her ankle and held it in one warm, strong hand. She pulled against him, but he tightened his grip.

"Miss Corwin, please," he said, a small laugh in the urgency of his voice. "We mean you no harm, I promise you."

Behind him, she saw the snow shovel begin a wide arc toward his head, but it was stopped by the intervention of a tall, older, gray-haired man.

"Whoa!" the man said, a hand to the handle her mother wielded with what had to be a painful grip for her. "Don't do that! I'm sorry we frightened you, but we just came to talk to Angelyn."

Angie felt the pulse in the younger man's thumb against her ankle bone, the warm strength of his grip as he stood over her awkward pose in the wheelbarrow, and was paralyzed for a moment. Curiously, fear was completely gone. What held her immobile was something different—a sense of significance...or discovery...or something she didn't understand but was just a little wary of.

Brandon continued to stare, because her face was everything they could have hoped it would be for camera close-ups. Her skin was creamy white and generously dusted with pale-gold freckles. Her cheeks were pink from their tussle, and her eyes—a magnificent true jade color—were bright with spirit and intelligence and, strangely, considering what had just happened, interest. Apparently in *him.*

"Interest" didn't begin to describe what *he* felt. Her hair had whipped across his face during their struggle, and he could still feel the touch of it on his cheek. Her ankle under his hand was slender, her vulnerable body in the wheelbarrow as tempting to him as any naked woman he'd ever seen.

Her eyes looked into his with a quality that probed and questioned, and weirdly made him want to spill his guts about all that had happened to him—his abominable childhood, his good fortune in crossing paths with Mike, his dreams for the future.

God. He never spilled his guts—not even to Mike. He freed her ankle, caught her waist in his hands and lifted her to her feet.

Then he stood there with his hands on her rib cage, oddly reluctant to let her go.

Her hands held his forearms where she'd clung for balance—and she didn't seem to want to let go, either. Her eyes continued to hold his.

Then the spell was broken abruptly when—in the sudden quiet of the musty shed—a female voice said in a startled, broken tone, "Mike?"

Brandon and Angie turned simultaneously to Angie's mother, who was still holding the shovel, and Mike, his hands on the handle, still preventing her from swinging it. Mike was looking down into a pair of shocked blue eyes, his own reflecting the same stunned surprise. "Gretta?" he asked.

Chapter Three

Angie watched in fascinated disbelief as her mother dropped the shovel and wrapped her arms around the tall, gray-haired man.

"Mike! Oh, Mike! How are you? And what are you doing *here?*"

"We're working on an ad campaign and needed a little peace and quiet to pull it all together." He pointed a finger in Brandon's direction, but brought that hand back to her shoulder immediately and pulled her into his laughing embrace again. "My God, I can't believe it! How come you're still here? You took off for Tanzania. How long ago was that?"

And suddenly, as quickly as the sparkle of reunion had begun, it was extinguished. Angie saw her mother flick a glance in her direction, then look back at the man she'd called "Mike" with a sudden stiffness in her tone and manner.

"Twenty-six years. So. Why did you come here? To this house?"

Mike studied her a moment, as though trying to assess the change in her. Then he said with quick courtesy, "Oh, not to impose upon you or anything. Brandon…'' Then suddenly, remembering he hadn't introduced him, he put a hand to his shoulder. "This is Brandon Prinz, my foster son and right-hand man at the company.''

Gretta nodded. "Rampion Pharmaceuticals. The family business. I remember.''

"The product we're working on is hair care," Mike went on, "and we've been through the photos of every modeling agency in L.A. and couldn't find the right woman to represent our product. Then Brandon spotted Angelyn.''

Gretta took a small step back. "How do you know her name?''

"We followed her into her tearoom, but she'd already gone out the back." He frowned again over her manner. "Her name's on the sign in the shop.''

Angie turned to the man who still held her waist, and realized with some surprise that she still held his arms. She dropped her hands and wrinkled her brow at him, not quite able to put all the pieces of this curious encounter together to make sense of it.

"You were following me…why?" she asked.

He smiled. He had nice dark eyes, a strong, straight nose and a beautiful mouth with straight, white teeth. The smile made him painfully handsome, but it had a curious quality about it—as though some emotional fence protected it.

"We wanted a closer look at your face," he replied candidly, "to see if it was a face we could use.''

"For what?''

"To sell shampoo.''

Angie didn't have the least interest in modeling anything for anybody, but she couldn't quite get over this odd convergence in her shed. Her mother had obviously once been friends with the older man, but that didn't seem to have anything to do with why he was here.

Now that she was convinced the men posed no threat, she felt her sense of common courtesy surface. And maybe she even owed the younger man an apology.

Then she remembered her instructions to her mother to call the police when she'd pushed her to the back of the shed.

"I don't think I'm model material," she said politely, sweeping a hand toward the open door. "But we can offer you a cup of coffee anyway." She smiled at Mike. "Apparently, you and Mother have a few things to catch up on."

Brandon watched Mike look from one woman to the other. "'Mother'?" he asked.

He was surprised that Mike hadn't already concluded the women's relationship from the physical evidence and from the way the young woman had presented herself as a fierce, if puny, defense, then by the way the older woman had come to *her* defense with the shovel. Of course, Mike had been distracted by this unorthodox reunion.

"Angie," Gretta began, trying to push her daughter toward the door. "I think these men need to be on their way. Why don't you..."

"Wait!" Mike said loudly, sharply.

Brandon braced himself, though he wasn't sure what for. Except that Mike never shouted. Even when they'd had rousing altercations when Brandon had been in his late teens, Mike had made all his points forcefully, but always quietly.

He watched Mike study Angelyn's face.

"Did you finally find a husband," he asked, without looking away from the young woman, "who'd travel from dig to dig with you, or did you give up archaeology for him?"

Angelyn placed an arm around her mother, who now looked pale and tense. "She never had to make the choice," she replied. "My father died in an auto accident just before I was born."

Oh, God. Brandon saw it coming. He didn't know whom to reach for first—Mike, who'd just gotten over a heart attack, or Angelyn, who still didn't seem to have a clue.

Her eyes were the same true-green color Mike's were, and she had a dimple in her left cheek when she smiled at him.

Brandon saw that same dimple appear in Mike's cheek as he inhaled sharply.

"How old are you?" Mike asked in a strangled tone.

"Twenty-five," she replied.

"When's your birthday?"

She frowned over the question, but answered it. "February 12."

Mike thought a moment, then put a hand to his heart and pressed there, as though to stop a pain. His jaw tightened and his eyes grew anguished.

Brandon covered the few steps between them in an instant and hurried to support him.

Mike, still staring at Angelyn, shook his head. "No. It's all right," he said thinly. "I have a pain in my heart, but it's not a heart attack."

Brandon watched excitement turn to sorrow in Mike's eyes, then sorrow turn to anger. Mike directed that angry gaze on Gretta.

"You had to have known you were carrying her when we parted," he said, his voice low and harsh with the pain he felt. He apparently failed to realize in his shock that Angelyn didn't have any idea what was happening. "How could you not tell me I had a daughter?"

Gretta put gnarled hands to her face.

Angelyn's eyes widened and she went completely still. "Daughter." She said the word not as a question, but flatly, as though it held no meaning for her.

For a moment, the four of them were frozen in a shaft of light in the old stone shed—Mike, with his tortured expression; Gretta, with her hands over her eyes; Angelyn, like a slender column of silence; and Brandon, thinking that there had to have been a face among all those photos that could have saved everyone from this point in time.

Then Angelyn turned her face toward her mother in a jerky, almost robotic movement. "This man is my father?"

Gretta didn't answer immediately and Angelyn turned her body suddenly, caught her mother's wrists and yanked her hands down. "Is he?"

Gretta winced, then looked into her daughter's face, her own pale with regret. "Yes."

Angelyn studied Mike for a long moment, her delicate features pinched into an expression of angry concentration.

Mike shook his head, his mouth quivering. Brandon, still holding his arms, tightened his grip.

"I didn't know," Mike whispered.

Angelyn studied him as though he were some revelation she couldn't quite understand. Then she made a plaintive little sound.

Mike reached a shaky hand out, but she drew back, her mouth contorting, and ran from the shed.

"Wait!" Mike shouted.

"Angie, let me..." Gretta cried, following her to the door. But she was gone.

Gretta turned back to Mike, her eyes alive with anger. "See what you've done!"

"What *I've* done?" Mike roared back at the same time that he pushed Brandon toward the door. "Go after her," he said urgently. "Make sure she's all right."

Brandon wanted to do that even before he'd been told, but he was worried about Mike. "Look, you're in an iffy state of stress right now," he said. "You should sit down, have a brandy. Maybe Angelyn just needs to be alone for a while."

"No," Gretta said, pushing on his other arm. "She's been alone too much of her life. Go. Go."

When Brandon hesitated, his concern for Mike still uppermost, she sighed and took Mike's arm in a gesture she intended to be solicitous but was still a little rough.

"I'll look after Mr. Subtle here. I'll even see that he sits down and has a brandy. Please," she added, anger slipping to show genuine concern. "Go after my daughter."

"'Our' daughter," Mike corrected.

Brandon left Mike and Gretta glowering at each other and took off after Angelyn. He didn't have a clue how to help her when she'd just had her entire life shattered like a tossed pumpkin. But he'd been asked to keep an eye on her, to make sure she was all right. He could do that. He hoped.

He ran to the edge of the yard, wondering which direction she'd taken. The Volvo was still there, so she'd set out on foot. He scanned the rim of woods that curved around the back of the cottage in a crescent shape and thought grimly that someone could be lost in there for days.

Then he caught a flash of red and white, and in the optimistic hope that they were her hair and her shirt, he set off at a run after the bright colors.

ANGIE FELT as though she was going to burst, and it wasn't simply for lack of air, as she ran for all she was worth through the trees. She was so filled with anger she didn't know herself. It raged inside her like something wild, like the thing in *Alien* that could burst out of her at any moment and eat whatever was near.

It was painful and unfamiliar and she hated it, but it fueled her, and right now she wanted more than anything to get as far away from the shed as she could.

She had a father! A father!

She ran away from the reality with the same desperation with which she'd wanted a father every moment of her life.

She remembered kindergarten as the time she'd noticed that all the other children had a man who came to school functions with their mothers. When she'd asked her mother where her father was, she'd explained that he'd died before she was born.

She remembered feeling jealous, deprived, cheated. And every time throughout her life when the situation had called for a father and she hadn't had one to produce, she'd felt the same way. She'd learned to accept it because she'd been astute enough to notice that nobody's life was perfect, but she'd hated it, had felt as though there was a locked door in her life and someone had thrown away the key.

She caught a spindly, second-growth tree trunk and fell against it, gasping for air, holding back a scream that sprang at her throat for release.

She hated screamers and whiners. She was going to handle this with dignity. She would hire a hit man to rub her parents out. Yes. That had a definite appeal. And while he was at it, she'd have him get rid of that quick-witted devil with the dark eyes who traveled with her father.

Her *father!* New pain bubbled up and she punched the side of her fist into the tree trunk.

She turned to lean her back against the tree and made an effort to get herself under control. She drew a breath, took it in deeply, then let it out slowly. She repeated the procedure, waiting for anger to diminish and for control to reestablish itself.

It didn't. She still felt furious and betrayed...and wanted to exact vengeance in ugly ways.

She tilted her head back to gulp in air—and saw

that she'd been followed. The man who'd tossed her around like a rag doll, who made her feel...what? She didn't know. She was too stressed at the moment to analyze it. The man her father...the man *Mike* had introduced as Brandon Prinz stood several yards away from her. He leaned a forearm against the trunk of a pine, the other hand on his hip as he caught his breath.

She jabbed a pointing finger in his direction. "Don't come near me!" she shouted.

He shook his head and raised a hand to indicate he had no intention of doing so. "Your parents," he said breathlessly, "just sent me to make sure you're okay."

"Well, you'd better send someone to make sure *they're* okay," she retorted, "because when I'm through with them, they're going to be sorry—" She stopped because he was smiling. It was that damned, beautiful, strangely protected smile, but how *dare* he?

"Tough guy?" he asked, folding his arms over his chest and leaning a shoulder against the tree. "You can't even accomplish a simple takedown with darkness and the element of surprise on your side."

She drew herself up in cold disdain. "So I was a failure. I intend to *hire* someone to work over my parents. And you, too, if you're not careful. Now, get out of my woods and leave me alone."

She turned away and set off at a brisk pace.

The shock was gone now, she noticed, but her anger was ripening and the need to scream and throw things was growing intense. She picked up a stick and whacked a tree trunk with it. She struck at ferny undergrowth, at a clump of gorse, then another tree trunk. She gave the stick an angry toss and concentrated on her footing as the terrain began to rise in a gradual slope.

Her slick-soled leather flats weren't designed for hiking, and the going became difficult. She leaned into the angle of the hill and pulled and pushed herself from tree to tree, still propelled by a need to keep moving. She'd climbed this hill the week she and her mother had moved into the cottage, and she knew there was a breathtaking view of a deep valley from the top.

She turned to find her pursuer still several yards behind her.

She held on to a low branch and shouted at him. "Go away. I'll be fine."

"Sorry," he shouted back. "I've been commissioned."

"Well, I *de*commission you."

"Good try, but you don't have the power to do that. How high are we going?"

"The top!"

"You going to make it in those shoes?"

She set off without answering to prove that she would. And she might have if she'd known there was loose rock under the carpet of pine needles. But she didn't. She stepped on it, lost her footing, fell onto her stomach with a cry of surprise and exasperation and began to slide down the hill.

She flailed for a handhold, expecting to break a leg at any moment in a collision with a tree. She felt helpless, a victim of that always alarming falling feeling one experienced just before sleep took over. Only she wasn't sleeping; she was awake. And her ignominious downward rush seemed like a metaphor for what was happening in her life. The grip she'd thought she had on everything was sliding down on its belly, out of control.

Her downward progress was halted suddenly when Brandon Prinz caught a fistful of her jumper skirt. She felt fingertips brush against her bottom as he tightened his grip. He was crouching with one arm around a tree trunk for balance as he hauled her toward him.

Angie wrapped an arm around his waist and literally climbed up his body until she had both arms around his neck. She held on to him fiercely as her shoes refused to gain purchase. She felt warm, hard muscle under her hands, his wiry hair against her temple.

Fine kettle of fish you've gotten yourself into, she began to scold herself, then discovered that in her belly flop down the hill, all the anger had left her, all the ability she'd thought she retained to contain her reaction had fled with it, and all she was left with was that need to scream and throw things.

But she couldn't possibly.

"Thank you," she said with what little dignity she could rescue, "for not allowing me to decommission you. Otherwise, I'd be at the bottom of the hill now with no nose and a rather crude appendectomy."

"It's okay," he replied quietly. She could feel the rumble of laughter in his voice right beside her ear, the warmth of his breath against her cheek. "Had you had a surfboard under you, your style would have been pretty good. You still want to get to the top?"

She did. Desperately. She needed something to do to stave off the need to sob. "Yes."

"All right. We're going to head off in that direction."

She held on to him but pulled back just enough to see him pointing off to the right.

"It'll be a little less steep that way, and the trees are thick enough to give us a lot to hold on to."

"Okay."

Their noses were an inch apart. She looked into his dark eyes and was surprised to find no recrimination there, just a quiet understanding she couldn't account for. But she was grateful enough for it not to question it.

"Ready?" he asked.

"Yes," she said.

The slope was much easier to deal with, she discovered, when one was being hauled up it by a sturdy hand. They gained the crest of the hill in five minutes and sat down at the top on a carpet of needles at the base of a very old pine.

Angie drew her knees up and, to her own horror, dissolved instantly into noisy sobs.

Brandon had no idea what to do for her, except that he could remember clearly how it had felt the first time Mike had put an arm around him in comfort. After years of loneliness and abuse, he'd thought himself pretty tough. But it had softened him, reassured him, and made him feel for the first time that he was no longer alone in the world.

He remembered Gretta's remark when she'd pushed him in pursuit of Angelyn. "She's been alone too much of her life," she'd said.

He put an arm around Angelyn's shoulders, prepared to be rebuffed, possibly even physically pushed away.

But she leaned into him, instead, and sobbed her heart out.

He rested his back against the tree, wrapped both arms around her and let it happen.

For those few moments his world seemed to be made up of wild auburn hair. It lay across his chest, was caught on his right sleeve and stroked like silk against his jaw as she wept.

On some other level, he was aware that his mind made no leap to business and the thought of what this magnificent hair could do for Rampion's advertising campaign. And it was more than sensitivity to her plight that held the thought away.

It was the fact that he was experiencing a personal involvement in the situation that he found mystifying. He'd felt it in the shed when he'd dumped her in the wheelbarrow, and he'd felt it on the slope when she'd clung to him for balance.

She'd needed him then for physical stability, but he'd had a feeling it was more than that. Just as his reaction to her was more than interest. It was a curious kind of fascination that he couldn't explain.

And women didn't generally fascinate him. He liked them; he squired them around town; he made love to them. But he found most women in business too dedicated to the struggle, and those he saw socially too dedicated to the "game."

This woman, however, ran a tea shop that served cakes with Irish whiskey in them, slung a garden hose over her shoulder as though she knew what to do with it and dealt with emotional trauma by climbing a mountain. She was a new experience for him.

He was also very much aware of the softness of her in his arms, of the side of one small, round breast pressed against him, the slender shoulder leaning into him for comfort. But he put those thoughts away, determined to find a way to explore them later.

For now, it was a curiously satisfying experience just to hold her.

He was sorry when she pulled out of his arms. Her hair swept across his hands and brushed the side of his face like a caress.

She tossed it behind her with a brisk flick of her hand and drew a deep breath. She looked at him with underwater-green eyes, her expression both resentful and grateful.

"I'm sorry," she said, wiping at her eyes with her fingertips. "I hate weepy women. You don't happen to have a handkerchief."

He produced a monogrammed white one from the side pocket of his cords.

She opened it out and held it to her eyes. "Thank you," she said. "You must have been brought up fastidiously."

He laughed; he couldn't help it. "Not exactly, no. Mike taught me to carry a clean handkerchief at all times. He said a man should always be prepared for a woman to get emotional."

She lowered the handkerchief, wrapped it over her index knuckle and dabbed at her nose. "Mike taught you," she repeated with a puzzled frown. Then she studied him speculatively for a moment, her eyes narrowing. "Oh, no. Are you my...brother?"

He thought he saw disappointment in her eyes. He liked that at first, then he decided he wanted to make sure he was putting the right spin on why she didn't seem to want to be related to him.

"First, tell me what you mean by 'Oh, no,'" he said.

"Just... Oh, no. Another life-altering surprise," she explained. "Are you?"

He still wasn't sure where that put him, but considering what she'd been through, he just let it go.

"No." He pulled his sweatshirt off because he noticed she was rubbing her arms. "Here. Put this on," he directed, and while she drew it over her head and tugged it into place, he told her briefly about how he and Mike had gotten acquainted.

He helped her pull her hair out of the neckline. It was heavy and silken and smelled of flowers. He suppressed a fervent desire to bury his face in it.

"You mean your own father," she said with a disbelieving tilt of her eyebrow, "just gave you up to him?"

Brandon tilted his head in a noncommittal gesture. "Not by choice. He went to jail for twenty years. Otherwise, I think he would have preferred to keep me around as an errand boy, a procurer of food and an outlet for his anger."

She looked horrified. "I'm sorry."

"Don't be." He smoothed down the collar of her shirt, which protruded from the neckline of his sweatshirt. "I have Mike. And now," he added gently with a rueful smile for the way she'd found out, "so do you."

She tucked her hands into the long sleeves and hunkered down into the shirt. Some of her earlier anger began to return now that the emotional release was out of the way. This would be the real stuff, he knew, and he hated to see it directed at Mike.

"Maybe I don't want him," she said.

He glanced up at her as he buttoned the cuffs of the long-sleeved shirt he'd worn under his sweatshirt. The wind on the hilltop had the bite of fall in it. "That, of course, is up to you. But having had him as a sort of father myself, I can tell you you'd be missing out on a lot."

"I've missed out on a lot for twenty-five years." Angie turned to look out at a green wooded valley spread out below them. Hawks circled, sun glinting off their wings. A narrow river wound its way along the undulating line of the foothills. Her tone was defensive. "I guess I can continue to get by."

"No, you can't."

She turned to him when he refuted her claim, her eyes sparking.

"Trust me," he said. "I didn't want any part of him, either. I'd made my way alone on the street for a long time. I had things my way and I liked not having to consult anyone about anything. But he smiled at me, always had a friendly word, tossed me an apple when I delivered his paper."

She smiled at that, however grudgingly. "From newsboy to corporate vice president. That's quite a success story."

He shrugged. "I'm not as proud of that as I am of my personal success. I stuck to myself, delivered Mike's paper when I knew he wouldn't be there, so I didn't have to deal with his efforts to take me to Children's Services, so that I could move in with him."

"Was your father in jail already?"

He nodded. "For a couple of months. I was living with this group of winos and another kid in a warehouse basement. But I discovered that I missed Mike. I missed getting a smile. I missed the kindness even more than the apple. Trusting him was a big step for me, but I did it. And that opened up the world for me."

Brandon was totally aware that much of that was a crock. He had learned to trust, but that extended only to Mike. And he didn't want him hurt by his daughter's rejection. And it was somehow important to him that she not be hurt anymore, either.

"Once you know people care about you," he said, "particularly if they need you, too, it's hard to get by without them."

"Why did Mike need you?" she asked.

"His wife died a couple of months before I got the paper route. And he didn't have any children." He gave her that rueful smile again. "At least, he didn't know he had. He was lonely."

"Had he been in touch with my mother," she began coolly, "after having carried on an affair with her for an entire summer, he might have found out."

"But she'd gone off to Africa, hadn't she?"

"Aren't there phones in…" she began, then realized that there might not have been twenty-five years ago. She sighed dispiritedly. "I can't believe my mother told me he was dead. That's an awful thing to do."

"Maybe," he suggested reasonably, "she thought it would be easier for you to think he simply wasn't there than for you to always wonder what he was like and why you never got to see him."

She huffed an indignant breath. "Whose side are you on?"

He thought about that and smiled. "I think I have a triangular take on this thing. Mike's an innocent victim, your mother, however misguided, probably thought she was doing the best thing for you and you have every right to be angry and upset."

She scrambled to her feet and glared down at him, her hands on her hips, the cuffs of the too-long sleeves flapping emptily. "How omniscient of you. You're the only one with nothing at stake in this little drama."

He had a feeling that wasn't entirely true. And he wasn't thinking about his concerns for Mike.

"Actually, I do," he corrected. "At least from a business perspective. You were going to get the hair-care products division of your father's pharmaceuticals company out of the hole."

The line of her shoulders softened. She resisted the interest that idea aroused in her for the space of a few steps as she walked around the tree under which he sat. Then she stopped in front of him. "Tell me about his company."

"It's called Rampion Pharmaceuticals," he replied, and gave her a brief rundown of what the corporation produced.

"Well, I don't understand why your sales are down," she said with genuine surprise. "You make the best shampoo on the market. I've been using it for years."

That was good news. He tried not to react, his mind working ahead to how perfect it would be for Mike to be able to become acquainted with his daughter while she modeled for Rapunzel.

"That's what my research showed," he agreed calmly. "So we decided to buff up our presentation, do some dramatic advertising, let everybody who's turned off by our old-fashioned packaging know that we're out there, that we have a new face and we're the best there is."

She walked around the tree the other way. "Good idea. Only the 'new face' will not be my face."

"I understand," he said.

She stopped in front of him. She had neat ankles. But then, he'd noticed that before when he'd held one. Still, it was safer observing that a second time than letting his eyes wander any higher. The skirt was long and voluminous, but the wind whipped it against her, outlining her knees, her thighs, the barely perceptible roundness of her stomach.

"I'll bet you don't," she said with a sigh, then turned to look out at the valley. "I'll bet you just think I'm being hysterical and unforgiving."

"Well, you're wrong. You have every right to be upset. I don't think it's wise, though, to make decisions when you're feeling emotional. I think you should wait until you feel more...at ease with the situation."

She sank to the ground again, a few feet ahead of him, her back to him. Her hair was... Well, there were no words.

"How do I learn to feel at ease with a father I've never seen, whom I thought was dead, who apparently didn't know anything about me and probably isn't thrilled by my existence, either?"

"The obvious answer," he replied, "is to get to know him, to let him get to know you. Maybe you'll both discover you share something wonderful. And maybe not. If not, you haven't lost anything you didn't have before this morning, have you?"

She was silent for a long moment. Then she propped a hand behind her and leaned on it to turn and look at him. "Is this part of your learning to trust principle? You can talk yourself into doing anything if you delude yourself into thinking the result won't hurt you?"

He met her gaze. "You don't delude yourself into thinking you won't be hurt. You recognize that you can live through being hurt, that you learn the outside limits of your own endurance—and *that* makes you able to take on anything."

"Look." She pivoted on the seat of her jumper to face him. She tucked her knees up beside her and dusted off her hands. "After years of living in the far reaches of the world, in lonely boarding schools, in downtown New York, where I didn't know a soul but the kitchen staff I worked with—I've finally got my little world just the way I want it. I have my mother, my tea shop and my own little house."

"And you want to bolt the door behind you," he guessed.

She resented the metaphor. "I don't want to hide. I just want to enjoy what I've wanted all my life and never had—my family. I know it's just two of us, but it's mine. And I want it. I don't want to make bold explorations that could rip it all up again."

"Well, you're passing up the opportunity," he said, sitting cross-legged so that he could lean closer to her in emphasis, "of getting your *entire* family together. There could be three of you."

She looked skeptical. "If he cared about her, he'd have stayed with her."

"Angelyn, you heard them! She didn't tell him she was carrying you."

It was alarming to hear her full name on his lips. No one ever used it. His baritone gave it a resonance that startled her.

"It's 'Angie,'" she corrected a little testily. "Just 'Angie.' And why does it have to be *her* fault?"

"I imagine it isn't anybody's fault," he said reasonably. "I think it just…happened."

"*I*…" she said, getting to her feet and angrily pointing a finger at the chest of his sweatshirt covering the bosom of her jumper, "just happened." She walked away from him into the trees, rubbing her arms, realizing for the first time that she hadn't been the result of her parents' love for each other, as she'd always been told, but rather an accident neither had intended nor probably wanted.

He pulled her to a stop and turned her around. "I think you should find out what happened," he said reasonably, "before you jump to melodramatic conclusions."

"Melodramatic?" she asked with deadly quiet. "You think my reaction is melodramatic?"

"Poor choice of words," he acceded immediately. "But when you're pretty much on your own at eight because your mother ran away years before, and your father's in and out of jail and doesn't give a rip about you anyway, the notion of having a mother who loves you and discovering you also have a father—and rejecting him because you're offended by how it happened—does seem a little...rash."

She considered that a moment, and decided grudgingly that he was right. But instead of being conciliatory, she asked darkly, "Are you always right? Tell me now, because I'm getting a little tired of it, and I can arrange to have you rubbed out, too, when I call the Mafia for a hit man."

He grinned. "I don't think they're in the Yellow Pages. I believe you have to have a connection who sets up a meeting in an empty garage or a back alley."

"Great. Do you have any such connections?"

"Do you think I'd tell you if I did, when you're intending to make *me* part of the contract?"

She raised an eyebrow. "Why not? What happened to learning about the outside limits of your own endurance?"

"You know, if I *were* your brother," he stated as he dusted himself off and started down the hill, "I wouldn't introduce you to any of my friends. You have entirely too much attitude."

"Wait!" she called, taking careful steps after him.

"Why?" he asked over his shoulder. "I don't have to, I'm *not* your brother."

Though she moved diagonally as he was doing, she still lost her footing in the flat shoes and ended up on her bottom this time. She skidded downhill, entangled him as he prepared to head in the other direction and caused him to fall in front of her. They bumped downhill as though riding a bobsled until he dragged them to a stop against a broad-trunked pine. He caught her arm as her body's momentum threatened to carry her past him.

"*That's* why you should have waited," she said breathlessly as she clung to him, her hair in her face, his sweatshirt and her jumper covered with pine needles and dirt. Then she thought she caught a glimpse of humor in his eyes and smiled thinly. "I'm sorry. Are you all right?"

"Oh, don't apologize," he said, getting to his feet with a wince and pulling her up after him. "When your hit men come for me, having spent this time with you will make broken kneecaps seem like a party."

"You're the one who chose to follow me."

"No, I didn't. Your parents sent me. Just goes to show you that nothing's gained by running away from difficult situations."

She made a scornful sound. "I think what this has shown us is that what goes up must come down. And if you're going to continue to insist that you're not my brother, please don't spout fraternal platitudes."

"Do you want me to leave you here?" he threatened.

"Go ahead," she retorted. "I'll just fall into you farther down the hill."

He looked heavenward in supplication. Mike was going to owe him for this. Big-time.

This was the area, he noted with relief, where the grade became more gradual. He could have left her and she'd have made it on her own, but he'd promised Mike.

And there was something in her that spoke to something in him. And now that he'd seen through a myriad of emotions from tears to fury, it was more than fascination. It didn't have a name yet, but he was a little afraid of what it could turn out to be.

He somehow knew that just as she'd done on the slippery slope, she'd knocked him down emotionally, gotten him entangled with her and was taking him along for a ride.

Chapter Four

"Do you want the eight-grain bread from the shop?" Gretta asked, her hand on the rolltop of the bread bin on the kitchen counter. "Or those hazelnut rolls?"

Angie, freshly showered and in a white apron with Tintagel Tearoom printed in blue letters on the front, carried two containers of homemade soup she'd just taken from the freezer. She gave her mother a dismissive look as she passed her.

"You decide," she answered, stopping at the stove, where a large saucepan awaited the frozen soup. "I'm not speaking to you."

Angie heard Gretta's sigh from behind her. There was the rustle of a plastic bag. "I think the men would like the rolls."

"Whatever."

"Shall I slice some cheese?"

"Whatever."

Gretta appeared at Angie's elbow, her face still pale, her eyes still anguished from the shocking revelation in the shed. "Angie, I know I did an awful thing. I know you're upset. Please let's talk about it."

"I'd rather give you the cold shoulder. I'm not ready to be sweet and forgiving yet."

Gretta dropped the bag of rolls on the counter beside the stove, then sank onto the small stool nearby. "You were never sweet and forgiving. Whenever I went to see you at school, or whenever you came home to the dig for the summer, you always fixed me with those judgmental green eyes that told me you weren't happy with me."

"I would explain to you that I wasn't happy with you," Angie said, taking a wooden spoon to break up the blocks of frozen soup, "because I missed you and I knew a visit only meant it would be harder when you went away again, or when I did. But I won't, because I'm not talking to you."

Gretta sighed and studied her in silence. Then she asked conversationally, "Wouldn't it be quicker to microwave that?"

"Yes, but I don't want to be quick. I need a little time before we all sit cozily around the kitchen table and discuss my father's sudden resurrection."

"I'm sorry. I know it'll be awkward, but I couldn't just demand that he leave. Once he got over the shock, Mike was rather...thrilled about you."

Angie cast her a dark glance. "I can think of a lot of times when I'd have been thrilled to know he existed. But I'm not sure now is one of those times."

"Well, too bad," Gretta said wearily, "because now is when you've found out."

"Thanks to you."

"Yes. Thanks to me. In the late sixties I was part of a new breed of women who had plans of their own.

In my case, it wasn't that I was excluding men—it was just that there weren't any young men willing to take off for the wilds of Tanzania to dig in the earth for fossils of Australopithecus.''

"And you weren't about to compromise."

"No, I wasn't," Gretta admitted. "I was twenty-one. I didn't understand then that life is all about compromise. I still thought I could live life my way and still have everything I wanted. Then I met your father.''

Angie turned the blocks of soup with the spoon as they began to soften. Interest was beginning to edge aside her anger. "So, did you really meet him here? Was that part of the story true?''

"Yes. Everything was just as I told you. I'd just gotten my degree and a place on Dr. John Borden's team at the Olduvai Gorge. I worked for the lodge as a waitress to earn money for my trip and incidentals, and Mike's family came to spend the summer at the lake.''

Angie heard her sigh. Her voice softened as she went on. "We met while swimming. He was underwater and grabbed my legs and dunked me, thinking I was his sister. He apologized with a bacon burger at the lodge, and we spent all of July and August together. He was smart and daring and liked it that I was smart and daring, too.'' She sighed again, but Angie thought she heard an edge of sadness in it this time. "You were conceived on a red plaid blanket in the reeds at the north edge of the lake. On the south side the Kiwanis were shooting off fireworks and the band was playing at the pavilion. But on our side, we were being reckless and foolish because we were very much in love.''

Angie could see them in her mind's eye, young and impassioned and forgetting to think about the consequences.

"I knew he was expected to take up a position in his father's company in Los Angeles in September," Gretta went on, "and he knew I had a plane ticket to Tanzania for the end of August. But we were in love and selfishly took what we could.''

Angie heard the pain in her mother's voice now. Wordlessly, she took the sherry she'd intended to add to the soup and poured Gretta a small glass.

Gretta accepted the wine in a gnarled hand, her eyes registering surprise at that consideration. She took a deep sip, closed her eyes and picked up the story. "The week before we were to part, Mike pleaded with me to change my mind and come with him." She smiled at Angie, a sorrowful shadow darkening her eyes. "I'd just found out about you several days earlier, and I was frightened. I almost said yes. But I knew what having a wife and a new baby would do to the career of a very young man being primed to take over a major corporation. And I knew that as much as I loved him, I'd always wonder if I'd have been the one to find the clue that would alter or confirm our theories on man's development.''

She downed the rest of the sherry and sniffed. Angie determined that the tears in her eyes were not from the wine, but from the memories.

"So, I told him it was best that we go our separate ways and find partners more suitable to the lives we'd chosen. He looked at me with those condemning green eyes.'' She fixed her blue gaze on Angie and straightened herself off the stool. ''The same look you gave me as a child. The same look you're giving me now.''

The soup was almost liquid now and simmering in the pot. Angie went to the refrigerator for the cheese, turbulent with emotion herself. ''Couldn't you just have explained that to me?'' she asked curtly as she took the cheese and a plate to the chopping block in the middle of the room. ''Why did you have to tell me he was *dead?*''

Gretta came to stand on the other side of the block. ''It was stupid. I know it was. But how does one explain that to a five-year-old when you're supposed to be surrounding her with a sense of security and permanence. 'I'm sorry, darling, your father and I had an affair, but we'd never be able to live together so I sent him away'? I don't think so.''

''Mom...'' Angie slammed the cheese grater on the block, her bottom lip trembling. ''I believed for twenty-five years that I had a father I would never ever be able to see. And he's right out there. I could have written him, talked to him on the phone, visited him. He could have come to visit *me.*''

Gretta came to put her arms around her. ''I know, Angie. I'm so sorry. But I swear, at the time I thought I was doing what was best for all of us. He didn't have to know about you and worry, and you didn't have to know you had a father but could learn to live without him. Knowing would have hurt you every day. This will only hurt for a while.''

Angie enfolded her mother in her embrace, deciding

that the issue wasn't that she, Angie, be satisfied with an explanation, but that they all find a way to proceed from here.

Over lunch, Mike had a suggestion on how that could be accomplished. He'd complimented Angie on her soup, on the hazelnut rolls and the tea brack he and Brandon had eaten in the shop.

"You're very skilled," he said. "I predict your tea-room will be an unqualified success. In a broader market like Los Angeles, you'd probably have a chain in no time."

Angie soaked up the praise and disregarded the Los Angeles reference, but the entire time she was thinking that no matter how hard she tried not to, she liked Mike Rampion's face. It was angular, with a nicely molded nose and chin; and his hair was white, but thick and side-parted, and made him look very distinguished. Every newly discovered father, she thought, should look just like him.

"Well," she said, trying hard to withhold any sign of approval. "Thank you. I'd just like to be able to make it here. Winter's supposed to be pretty difficult."

"I'm sure if you cultivate their loyalty with good food, the locals will support you when the travelers stop coming through."

"That's what we're hoping." Gretta said. "And I'm going to write a book, so that'll help."

"About your experiences?" Brandon asked. He'd taken a shower after Angie, and Gretta had washed his clothes. Angie let her eyes run over the sweatshirt he'd lent her and that he now wore again, remembering how warm it had felt against her bare arms, how it had protected her from the mountaintop chill.

He looked away from her mother and caught her watching him. She picked up the coffee warmer and refilled his cup and Mike's to divert his attention. "Mom was looking at her diaries and maps the other day," she said chattily, "and thought it would be a good idea to try to put some ideas together and contact a publisher."

"I know an agent," Mike said with enthusiasm. "Golf with him every Tuesday. When you're ready, he can help you. I'll give you his number."

Gretta looked both startled and pleased. "Thank you," she said.

He glanced down at his cup suddenly, picked it up by the tips of his fingers, turned it ninety degrees, then put it down again. "Or better yet," he said, looking up with that same casual expression, the same easy tone of voice, "you can come back to L.A. with us and talk to him yourself."

"Mike Rampion," Gretta said with sudden vehemence, "you are like talking to a wall. Neither Angie nor I is going to Los Angeles, so forget it."

Angie presumed that meant her mother and Mike had discussed the subject while she and Brandon had been absent. She was inclined to agree that she wasn't going anywhere, but considering that her mother had made several major decisions about Angie's life when Angie had been too small to question them, she took a certain satisfaction in questioning those decisions now.

"Go to Los Angeles?" she asked, ignoring her

mother's harrumph of displeasure. "For the hair thing, you mean?"

Mike turned to her, his manner gentling, as though she were five instead of twenty-five. "You can do that if you like or not," he said. "Whatever would make you happy. I'd just like to spend some time with you now that I've found you. And your mother, of course."

The nugget of an idea was beginning to form.

"What would I have to do?" she asked, looking away from her mother and focusing on her father.

He shrugged. "Just be beautiful. A few of your days in front of the camera might be long, but we'll make up for that by buying you a wardrobe for the shoot and taking you around town to relax you at the end of the day. And I have a comfortable place in Beverly Hills."

Beverly Hills? She withheld a gasp. "How long would it take?"

He consulted Brandon, who sat at a right angle to him. "A week," Brandon replied. "Maybe ten days."

Now for the all-important question. "What does it pay?" she asked.

Mike looked a little taken aback, but he replied, "Union scale." Then he named a figure that astonished her. "Plus wardrobe and expenses."

She cleared her throat, trying not to appear naive. "All right," she said. "I'll do it."

"Michelle Angelyn, what is wrong with you? You have a shop to run that's only been open a month!" her mother reminded her sharply. "Becky cannot run it by herself, and I can't be much help with these..."

She held her gnarled hands up as if to stress the point of her clumsiness around crockery and the coordination required in the kitchen. Then, though Angie looked quickly away, Gretta obviously saw what she'd tried so hard to hide.

She was out of her chair in an instant, shaking a crooked finger over her daughter while Mike and Brandon eyed each other in puzzlement.

"No!" she said. "You will not do this! You are not going to L.A. to make money to pay to have my hands done!"

"Hands done?" Mike asked.

"There's a surgical procedure," Angie said, pushing her mother gently aside so that she could see Mike, "that would make her hands much more functional and ease her discomfort considerably. But it costs a bundle. Her health insurance won't cover it."

"Well, please don't worry about that," Mike began. "I'd be happy to pay for any..."

Out of the corner of her eye, Angie saw the quick and subtle shake of Brandon's head, and the warning expression that turned to one of innocence when she gazed at him.

She warned him with a look to stay out of her affairs, then turned to her father with a briskness intended to abort his offer and keep her mother out of it.

"I can take care of us," she said.

"You are *not* going to do this!" Gretta said loudly.

"I am," Angie insisted with an imperious look she learned from an oil heiress at boarding school. "And you're coming with me."

Gretta folded her arms. "I am not."

Angie shrugged. "Well, suit yourself. In fact, Becky's husband is doing his reserves training for the next few weeks. I'll ask her to stay with you at night."

"And what about the shop?"

"I have a lot of things made ahead and frozen. And the fancy things that need decorating, Becky can try her hand at. If that doesn't work, she can just explain to my customers why I'm away. I imagine they'll find it forgivable. I'll have a grand opening when I come back, serve great stuff and reestablish rapport with my clientele."

Mike studied her from across the table, his eyes unashamedly filled with emotion. "You have a good business head as well as a will of iron," he noted.

Gretta rounded on him. "She got all her bad qualities from *you!*"

He met her angry accusation with equanimity and a look that spoke of what they'd once shared. Despite Angie's and Brandon's presence, Mike's smile for Gretta was intimate. "Is that why you named her Michelle?"

GRETTA STAYED in the house when Angie walked Mike and Brandon out. Mike caught Angie's arm and stopped her at the top of the driveway as Brandon went on to the car.

"I don't mean to cast blame on your mother," Mike said, the late-afternoon sun brightening eyes that were just like those she faced in the mirror every day. "I'm sure she thought what she did was right, but I want to make sure you understand that I didn't have a clue you were on the way. I'd *never* have left you without support or money for your education. I'd never have left you at all!''

She found it exciting to look up at the tall, stalwart man and know that she was a part of him. He seemed to be kind and compassionate; that was also nice to know.

''Mother took good care of me,'' she assured him.

''She said you lived with her at the dig until you were ten, then she sent you home to boarding school— and that you hated it.''

''Mostly I hated being away from her. I went back to the dig for summers, but I just always felt that something was missing in our lives.'' She narrowed her eyes against the sun and smiled up at him. ''I guess it was you.''

His eyes brimmed and he pulled her against him in a firm hug. She felt the strength and the tenderness in him she'd so longed for as a little girl and let herself take them in, savor them, store them.

''So.'' He tucked her into his arm and started toward the car. ''We intended to head back in two days. Do you want to ride with us, or shall I make a plane reservation for you?''

''Well…'' She looked at Brandon, who was leaning patiently against the car door, arms folded, sunglasses shielding his eyes, and knew with some high-frequency instinct that he was going to be trouble. She found him handsome, interesting, even caring—and at any other moment in her life that would have been a road worth exploring.

But not now. One life-altering experience at a time was about all she could handle.

But if she chose not to go, her father would construe it as rejection, and there wouldn't be money for her mother's surgery. So she really had little choice. But she was going to have to be careful.

"I won't be intruding upon the male-bonding thing?" she asked as they approached the car.

Brandon straightened, an eyebrow raised at her question.

"No," Mike said with a laugh. "Brandon and I bonded long ago." To Brandon he explained, "She wondered if she'd be intruding if she rode home with us rather than flying."

"'Course not," he replied, pulling his door open, his grin teasing under the masking sunglasses. "When we get to the freeway, she can drive."

Her father hugged her again. "Ignore him. He has a brutal sense of humor." He drew her away and looked into her eyes, his expression serious. "I left you the address and the phone number of our place." She nodded. "I imagine your mother won't appreciate my showing up again, so if you need me before we leave, please call or come over. Otherwise, we'll pick you up here Friday morning, all right?"

"Yes. Thanks."

Angie shaded her eyes and watched them back out of the driveway and turn toward town. She had a father, she thought in wonder.

"I HAVE a *daughter*," Mike said as the beautiful, wooded countryside sped past the windows of the car.

"My God! A *daughter*."

Brandon gave him a diagnostic glance. "Do you feel all right? I think I should run you into Redding just to make sure the shock hasn't done you any harm."

"I'm fine," Mike replied, leaning back against the headrest and closing his eyes. "I have a daughter." He opened his eyes again suddenly and rolled his head on the seat rest so that he could look at Brandon. "This doesn't affect the love and affection I have for you. I don't want you to think..."

"I don't," Brandon interrupted him instantly. "Honestly. I don't."

"You're my son in every way that matters."

"I know that."

That issue resolved, Mike closed his eyes again and smiled. "Isn't she the prettiest thing?"

Brandon saw the time he'd spent with her that morning run through his mind like a videotape. He could even pause on the moments that his brain had isolated and stored—the moment when she'd stood on the post-office steps and the wind had tossed her hair into a billowing cloud of dark fire; the moment when she'd looked up at him from the depths of the wheelbarrow and he'd seen in her eyes that she felt the same sense of recognition he'd felt; the moment when they'd crested the hill and she'd dissolved into tears in his arms; the moment on the way back down the hill after they'd argued, when she'd slid down the hill, dumped him on his butt and come up dusty and disheveled and grudgingly apologetic.

"Yes," he replied casually. "Very pretty."

"She's perfect for the ad."

"Perfect."

"And she's my *daughter!*"

"I think we've established that."

"Her mother was like that, you know." Mike sat up and stretched his arms as though he were too restless to be confined by the car.

"Like what?" Brandon asked.

"Independent, a little superior..." There was a smile in his voice. "With a tendency to think she knew it all. I found that very sexy because my life was planned for me. I didn't have to make enormous decisions and succeed or fail because of them."

"You've done that many times over since then."

"Yeah. I guess. But she was just twenty-one when I drove her to Sacramento and put her on a plane to begin her long journey to Tanzania. I was angry at her for not wanting to stay with me, but deep down, I admired her ability to do what she damn well pleased." He sighed and opened his window. "I just wish that hadn't included keeping my child from me."

"I imagine she knew if she told you, you'd have felt obliged to go with her, or tried to make her stay with you—and that wouldn't have been good for either of you."

"So instead, my daughter grew up without me." He drew in a deep gulp of air. "It isn't fair that she's the one who paid the price."

"Well, now you'll have ample opportunity to make some of it up to her."

Mike's mood lightened at the thought. "We'll put her in that guest room overlooking the garden."

"Maybe I should move out while she's with you," Brandon suggested, turning onto Lakefront Drive. "You'll want some privacy and I'll..."

"No. You moved back in after my heart attack to keep an eye on me," Mike reminded him, shamelessly working guilt into his argument. "And I've come to count on having you around. The house is big enough to hide Disneyland. You won't be in the way. Besides, we do some of our best brainstorming over brandy at night."

"She might want you to herself."

"She's not very sure of me yet. I think she'll appreciate the buffer. You're staying."

"All right. Take it easy." Brandon pulled into their driveway, then neatly into the garage attached to the house.

"Let's take a walk around the lake and go to Wah Mae's for dinner," Mike suggested, climbing out of the car.

Brandon looked at him doubtfully. "I think you should rest for a while. This morning had to be a blow to your system."

"No, I'm too antsy to rest. If I get tired or don't feel well, we'll come back." He hooked an arm around Brandon's shoulders and drew him with him around the house and down the trail toward the lake. "I want to know what you thought of her. Did you like her? Is she somebody you could see every year at family get-togethers and still look forward to the next one?"

"Yeah," Brandon answered, thinking wryly to himself that that didn't begin to cover what he felt for Michelle Angelyn Corwin.

"MAYBE WE COULD get a group of survivalists to stay with your mom," Becky suggested. The shop was closed and Becky wiped off tables while Angie polished the glass on the display case. "They know how to get through difficult situations and they're, you know, armed."

Angie replaced the cakes she'd moved from above the case, securing their protective tops. She tossed her cloth aside and leaned her forearms on the case to study Becky sympathetically. "I can make other arrangements if you think it'll be too trying."

The last table wiped off, Becky came to face Angie across the display case. She grinned. "No, I promised and I'll do it. I'm just teasing. I'm sure your mother and I will get along fine."

"And you can take care of everything here with your sister coming in to help out?"

"No problem." Becky rolled her eyes as she pulled off her apron. "I can't believe you're going to be the star of an advertising campaign. Just like Isabella Rosellini!"

Angie followed Becky into the kitchen. "Hardly like Isabella Rosellini. My mother wasn't Ingrid Bergman."

"No. She's more like Humphrey Bogart. Just kidding!" she decried instantly when Angie berated her with a look of theatrical indignation. "Your shop and your mother will be fine, I promise. Just have a great time. I was so sure those two men meant you harm, and they turn out to be your long-lost father and sort-of...brother."

Angie tossed their aprons into the laundry and handed Becky her blue cotton jacket. "No, Brandon keeps insisting he's not my brother."

Becky waggled her eyebrows. "Because he'd probably like to be something else to you."

"I don't think so." Angie pulled on a dark green cotton jacket that matched her slacks, knotted and shouldered the plastic bag of laundry and picked up her purse. "I think he just doesn't want anything to do with me. We kind of got into it when he followed me up the hill."

Angie and Becky made their way past tables in the now-shadowy tearoom to the front door. "But you said he let you cry on his shoulder," Becky reminded her. "And got you down the hill again."

Angie turned the sign to Closed, opened the door and followed Becky through it. The sun was low, the bright late afternoon just beginning to purple with dusk.

Angie locked the door behind them, then turned her key in the alarm plate to activate it.

"He didn't really *let* me cry on his shoulder. I just did it. And he helped me down the hill in self-defense, because I kept knocking him down when I fell and slid into him."

"Hmm," Becky said. "Well, if he doesn't want anything to do with you, what is he doing here?"

"What?" Angie turned away from the alarm to see Becky pointing unobtrusively to the bookstore next door, which was also closed. Brandon Prinz perused the window display of current bestsellers, hands in the pockets of black slacks. He turned toward them at the sound of her voice.

Becky gave him a quick wave, then turned to Angie, her hand held out.

Angie felt momentarily flustered by his presence. He looked tall and elegant in a casual gray sport coat over a black turtleneck, but definitely out of his element in Gray Goose Lake. And he had that way of looking at her as though he knew things about her even she didn't know.

She looked back at Becky, confused about what she wanted.

"The keys." Becky took the little gold cup-and-saucer fob that dangled from Angie's key chain and plucked the ring from her grip. "You're leaving in the morning, remember. I have to open up." Then she added in a whisper intended for Angie's ears alone, "You may think he doesn't want anything to do with you, but we both know *you* feel differently, don't we?"

Angie focused sufficiently to elbow Becky as she passed her.

"See you in a couple of weeks," Becky called over her shoulder as she moved toward a little white Toyota parked at the end of the block. She raised her voice a little and shouted instructions to Brandon. "You send her back safely!"

He waved a hand at her. "I will." Then he turned his attention to Angie and smiled as he closed the distance between them. "You running away to sea?"

he asked, indicating the bag over her shoulder. "Or are you practicing early to be Mrs. Santa?"

She dropped the bag to the sidewalk. "Laundry," she explained briefly, a little unsettled by what he was doing there alone. "Is...Mike all right?"

"He's fine," he said, picking up the sack of laundry. "I thought it'd be a good idea for us to talk before we head home tomorrow. Can I take you to dinner?"

She was both panicked and intrigued by the idea, but pleased to have an excuse. "I have to fix dinner for my mother," she said, trying to take the bag back from him.

He held it away from her. "Mike's taking her out."

She narrowed her gaze on him suspiciously. "I don't believe that. She wouldn't go."

"She did," he insisted. "They're at that little Chinese place. He called me on his cell phone and asked me to let you know so you wouldn't worry."

"Why didn't he call me himself?"

"He tried. Your line was busy."

She thought back and remembered that Becky had spent a little while on the phone with her sister while they had a three-way conversation nailing down details of their duties while Angie was gone.

"What is it?" he asked, studying her expression. "Are you afraid of me suddenly?"

She was, curiously, but not in the way he meant. "Of course not," she denied. "It's just that the past few days have produced some startling surprises. I thought maybe you had another one."

"I assure you, Angie," he said with a rueful grin, "that though you've only had him a day and a half, your father would kill anyone who hurt you, even me. So, no, I have no surprises. Just a caution.''

Now, that sounded alarming. ''About what?''

He held up the large bag to indicate its awkwardness. ''I thought we could go to that burger place up the street. But Mike's got the car. Can we put this in your car and walk up? Or do you want to drive?''

She looked up at the darkening sky, a sliver of moon already visible over the lake. The evening was fragrant with leftover summer and the promise of fall. It was a time made for lovers. That thought caused a vivid little ripple of sensation in her chest.

''All right, we'll walk,'' she said, crossing the sidewalk to her car and unlocking the door. He handed her the bag and she pushed it into the back, then closed the door and turned to him. ''But what do we need to talk about?''

''Us,'' he said.

Chapter Five

"Us?" she asked.

They'd walked the three blocks in relative silence, ordered a cheese-and-bacon burger for him and a plain burger for her and decided to share an order of onion rings. They now sat across from each other in a dark blue, molded Formica booth, the steaming, fragrant food on the table between them.

He snagged the salt and pepper shakers in one hand and the ketchup in the other and placed both beside the baskets of food.

"You and me," he said, glancing up at her as he unwrapped a straw and jabbed it efficiently into the plastic lid on his drink. "I want us to be clear on something."

She'd been busily spreading mustard from a foil packet onto her burger when he spoke. She looked across the table at him and he saw her curious expression turn to hurt feelings, followed by disappointment, followed by a very ripe anger.

Before he could calculate what that procession of emotions could indicate, she gave him a look that could have withered the outer skin of the space shuttle and said, "I have no intention of diluting your inheritance, if that's what concerns you."

Brandon wasn't sure how he resisted beaning her with the ketchup bottle. The good manners Mike had ingrained in him, he guessed.

He did take satisfaction in picking up the ketchup bottle, snapping off the cap with an angry twist and sweeping the food aside to lean closer to her and ask ominously, "Would you like to wear several ounces of this?"

She looked uncertain for an instant; then he was happy to see that gamut of emotions reverse itself in her eyes.

She drew a breath. "I'm sorry. It seemed like the kind of thing you might be concerned about."

"Well, I'm not. I thought I explained to you yesterday when I got you up *and* down the hill that Mike is the most important person in my world."

"You did," she agreed quietly.

"Then you owe me an apology."

"I already apologized once."

"Once won't do it for that remark," he said.

"Okay!" she said with an impatient stress on the word. "I apologize up and down. This is all very new to me and you say you want to talk about us, and I can't imagine how we relate to each other sufficiently to create a subject—except in the matter of Mike."

"I did want to talk about Mike—but the man, not his money." He turned the ketchup onto his onion rings. Nothing came out.

Angie reached across the table to take the bottle from him. "You have to get some air into it," she said, holding it over his onion rings and banging it against the side of her fist. A blob of ketchup came out and she quickly righted the bottle. "That enough?"

"Yes, thank you," he said, impressed with her skill.

"So, what about Mike?"

He would have felt guilty bringing up the subject in view of her vehement denial a moment ago, but he wouldn't be comfortable about Mike's emotional safety until he knew for sure.

She looked up at him, waiting.

"I want to be sure," he said frankly, "that you aren't coming to L.A. out of revenge."

That withering expression crossed her face again. "Revenge?" she asked quietly.

"Revenge," he repeated, looking back at her intrepidly. "You talked about it on the hill. I want to make sure you've gotten over that initial burst of anger and that it was just talk. Just as he'd kill anyone who'd hurt you, I'd decimate anyone who hurt him. I thought you should be warned."

Her eyes became explosive. "Well, thank you, Henry Kissinger," she said roughly under her breath, picking up the ketchup bottle and ripping the lid off, "for that excellent piece of diplomacy. How dare you get all indignant when I suggest you have money in mind, then turn around and accuse me of vengeance?"

He shushed her, looking around to see if anyone had noted her outburst. But the only other patrons were a young couple with three small children, who were too preoccupied to even glance away from their own table.

"Easy," he said quietly, raising a placating hand. "I just wanted to be honest."

"You wanted to be suspicious," she accused.

He looked directly into her eyes. "Didn't you?"

She stared him down for a long moment, then put the ketchup down with a bang. "I'm going to Los Angeles to get to know my father and to earn money for my mother's surgery. I imagine this will disappoint you, but you don't have to kill me after all."

He smiled amiably. "Good. Then I'll do my best to see that you have a great time."

The tension eased somewhat, she picked up her burger and frowned at him over it. "For that, you'll have to let someone else show me around."

"Truce." He handed her several napkins off the tray, then turned to put the empty tray behind them. He smiled into her eyes when he turned back again. "Now that I know you don't mean Mike any harm, I promise to be charming."

"And I'm expected to believe that you can?"

"'Course not. I'll prove it to you."

She was surprised when she dropped him off at just before eight that night that he had managed to do that. With the issue of Mike's sanctity settled between them, he told her about life in Los Angeles and all the things Mike had talked about showing her.

Wanting to do her part to restore an emotional balance between them, she listened intently, tried to share in his enthusiasm, and was surprised to find that she didn't have to try too hard.

Mike was home when they arrived, and he came out

of the house to greet her when he heard the car in the drive.

"I understand you took Mom out to dinner," Angie said as he leaned down to look at her through the driver's side window. The porchlight illuminated his wry expression.

"Yes," he said. "We started fighting over what to have for appetizers and it went downhill from there. She was always headstrong and bossy, but she's gotten even worse."

Angie explained how much her mother had loved her work, and that the arthritis now made it impossible.

"She hates being dependent on me," she defended, "though I'm delighted to finally have her around on a regular basis—even as cranky as a she-bear. I think her plan to put a book together will help."

"I wish she'd come to L.A. with us," he said.

Angie shook her head. "Once she makes up her mind, you can't budge her."

He laughed grimly. "No one knows that better than I." Then he patted her arm that was resting on the open window. "Sleep well tonight. We'll pick you up at seven."

"I'll be ready."

"BECKY WILL BE HERE to fix breakfast and dinner," Angie said, repeating everything they'd discussed over the past few days because her mother tended to ignore her every time she mentioned the trip, and she was afraid some of the details hadn't gotten through to her. And Mike and Brandon were picking her up in ten minutes. "I've frozen some lunches for you, but I put them in plastic bags so you don't have to mess with lids." Even a plastic lid could be hard for her swollen knuckles to deal with. "Just microwave the bag, then if you have trouble opening it, pass it through that snipper blade on the can opener."

"I'm not deaf." Gretta looked out the window at the frail morning light. Over her shoulder, Angie could see that beyond the kitchen window the tall grass in the field across the road swayed in the early-morning breeze, the daisies were bright around the base of her apple tree, and the mountainscape beyond the window craggy against the blue sky. It would be another beautiful day. "You told me all this yesterday. And last night. I'm arthritic, not incompetent."

"You're also unresponsive and pouty," Angie said, moving her two bags from the hallway to the front door, "so I don't know if you're listening to me or not."

Gretta turned away from the window, the set of her jaw defensive, the look in her eyes troubled. She was in a curiously fatalistic mood Angie wasn't familiar with.

"What if you decide you like Los Angeles?"

Angie studied her, analyzing what the question meant. "Are you afraid I'll decide to stay?"

Gretta shrugged a shoulder, a slender, almost fragile figure in her jeans and sweatshirt, and went to the coffeepot. Angie had tied her hair back for her in a clip, because her hands hadn't been able to manage the simple mechanism.

"That isn't impossible, is it?" Gretta asked, carefully pouring a cup. "You loved New York, and L.A.'s probably like that—big and cosmopolitan."

"I don't think L.A.'s anything like New York," she replied, startled and a little upset that her mother seemed to be worried that she would lose her. She felt like a mother herself, leaving a child at a baby-sitter's for the first time. "And you and my tearoom are here. I'll be back in a week."

"But what if you like it?"

"I'll still be back in a week."

Gretta sipped her coffee and crossed to the window to look out again at the morning. "What if you like him?"

For a minute, Angie suspected her mother had noticed her strong, but inexplicable, reaction to Brandon.

Then Gretta clarified pensively, "No one knows better than I how charming he can be. And that he's honest and genuine and...wonderful. If a little inclined to like things his own way."

She was talking about Mike.

Gretta sighed, her back still to Angie. "What if he wants you to stay?"

Angie went to the window and wrapped her arms gently around her mother's back. "You know," she said gently, "I think you're using the way I might react to him as an excuse. I think now that you've seen him again, you're wondering what your life would have been like if you'd found a way to make it work between you."

"I couldn't have worked here," Gretta returned simply. "And he couldn't have come with me. What's done is done." She turned to touch Angie's face with twisted fingers. "I do regret that I've hurt you. You understand that, don't you?"

"Yes."

"And it's not that I don't want you to get to know him, to learn to love him. I just..." She sighed and winced as though something hurt. "You're everything to me, Angie. I want you to do what will make you happy. I guess I'm thinking that I probably do deserve to lose you."

"Mom..." Angie dropped her hands from her mother's waist, tempted to shake her and knowing that wasn't advisable. "You're not going to lose me. I'll be back with money for your surgery. And things will go on as they have been, except that you'll have better use of your hands and I'll know what it's like to have a father."

Gretta's eyes were pitying, as though Angie was naive to think anything could be as it had been before. Then she closed her eyes for an instant, and when she opened them again, the mood was gone.

"You'd better find something else to do with the money," she said, "because you're not using it to pay for my surgery."

Angie groaned. "Don't start with me, Mom."

"Here comes your father." Gretta shooed her to the door, and though she couldn't help with the bags, she scooped up Angie's coat and followed her out the door as the Lexus pulled up into the driveway. "Now, remember, soft-pedal your bad habits. You'll be sharing a place with two men who might not be as crazy about George Strait as you are. And just because *I* let you change the channel when I'm watching wrestling, it doesn't mean they will. And for heaven's sake, don't go into one of your tirades on catch-and-release fishing. Most people consider it harmless.''

Angie stopped halfway to the car and turned to confront her mother, secretly relieved that the morose mood was gone. Or at least that she was pretending it was.

''Is there anything else?'' Angie asked wryly.

''Yes.'' Gretta lowered her voice as the men climbed out of the car and approached. ''Keep your Democratic politics to yourself. And sit up straight when you get in front of the camera. You're not exactly Dolly Parton, you know.''

''Good morning.'' Mike looked fresh and robust in gray slacks and a red sweater.

Brandon had walked around the car to open the trunk and now came toward them, moving with easy grace in jeans and the sweatshirt he'd lent her two days earlier.

Angie felt her pulse quicken, her body tense as though bracing to take action. It occurred to her that she was experiencing a reaction to danger.

''Ladies,'' Brandon said with a smile that encompassed her mother and her. Then he leaned close to her and she took a step back.

He noted her reaction with a moment's hesitation and the arch of an eyebrow. ''Your bags?'' he asked.

He wanted her bags. Not her. She maintained her poise with a deep breath. ''Of course,'' she said, setting them down.

With a quick, chiding glance at her, he picked up the bags and took them to the car.

"You're sure you won't come with us?" Mike asked Gretta. "We can wait for you to pack a bag. Your arthritis might be happier in a warmer climate."

Gretta shook her head. "Thanks, but I'll keep an eye on things here."

"You're sure? Lots of museums in L.A. with lots of antiquities."

"No. I've been too long in the bush. This is as close to civilization as I want to get."

"All right. But don't worry about Angie. Brandon and I will take good care of her, and I'll see that she calls you."

Gretta smiled. "Don't worry about that. Just see that she has a good time."

"We will." Then Mike surprised Gretta with a quick hug. "Take care." He took a card from his sweater pocket. "This has all my numbers—home, office, fax, pager. Call anytime, day or night."

She accepted it in her misshapen hand. "Thank you."

Mike gave Angie a quick squeeze. "Say goodbye to your mom and let's get on the road."

Angie watched him walk away, thinking that had been a very paternal remark. Then she turned back to her mother, her heart seized with sudden worries.

"You're sure you'll be okay?"

Gretta linked her arm in Angie's and walked her slowly toward the car. "I'll be fine. You just watch out for you. And try not to act like such a geek in front of Brandon. He's gorgeous. He seems to be thoughtful. And if he's worked with your father all these years, he's probably got a bundle."

Angie stopped in her tracks to point a finger at her. "You..."

But Gretta caught her in a hug. "Have fun, don't worry, but remember to come home."

Angie protested when Mike urged her into the passenger seat in the front. Brandon had climbed into the back.

She ducked down to look in at him. "Do you have enough leg room back there?" she asked. "Why don't you sit up front? I'd be fine in the back."

He indicated the briefcase on the seat beside him. "I've got work to do, and Mike'll want to talk to you."

"You're sure?"

"Yes. After lunch we'll play musical seats because Mike makes me drive through Sacramento, and I'll need him to copilot. But for now, you're fine up there."

And they were off with a wave and a honk of the horn for Gretta.

BRANDON DIDN'T have work to do, but he wanted Mike to have Angie beside him. He hadn't considered having the bonus of the view of the back of her head, until she settled in front of him. She'd woven her hair into a braid for the trip, but the thick, auburn-colored skein gleamed in the sunlight. Wisps of the stuff curled at her ears and along her nape.

He decided that he should find something to do just to keep his eyes off her.

He looked over the notes he'd taken on Mike's brainstorming for the hair-products campaign, but had difficulty concentrating on them when the subject of the campaign was directly in front of him, her floral fragrance drifting back to him.

Angie listened quietly for much of the morning while Mike talked nonstop about working with his father after Gretta left for Africa, about meeting Ruthie in a disabled elevator in their office building and sitting on the floor with her for three hours until they were finally freed.

Then he told her all the things he'd told Brandon over the years—how he and Ruthie had been friends as well as lovers, how she'd developed a heart problem fairly early in their marriage and how it had prevented them from having a baby or even being able to adopt.

"She'd have loved the two of you," he said, glancing away from the long, empty ribbon of Interstate 5 to smile at Angie, then into the rearview mirror at Brandon.

"I never forgot your mother," he went on to Angie, "but I...got on with my life. As she did. Tell me what it was like for a little girl on an archaeological dig."

"It was wonderful when I was small," Angie replied. "There were children of other families on the dig, as well as native children to play with. We had acres on which to play, all kinds of things to explore." The cheerful tone of her voice altered slightly. "When I came back to the States for boarding school, I found it hard to adjust to the different life-style, to children who'd grown up so differently. I was lonely."

Mike put a hand out to her, the expression Brandon

could see only in profile reflecting the regret he must have felt that he hadn't been there for her.

"Then I discovered cooking." The cheerful note returned to Angie's voice. "And through it, I discovered a lot about myself. I also acquired friends who'd kept their distance before because we had so little in common." She laughed philosophically. "People will forgive you almost anything if you can make a great chocolate cake."

Mike laughed, too, but Brandon studied the fragile line of Angie's neck and realized that he and she had a lot more in common than it first appeared. Loneliness felt the same, no matter what prompted it.

"I won a cooking contest," Angie said, "and the prize was a scholarship to a culinary school. I worked for four years at Tuxedo Junction, the dining room of the Starbury Hotel in New York's theater district, and loved the rush and excitement of it. Then a colleague of Mom's called me, because Mom had just gotten the verdict that she couldn't work anymore and didn't intend to tell me."

Mike made a sound that suggested he wasn't surprised. "That's Gretta."

"Unfortunately for her, I've inherited a few of her qualities. I went to Tanzania and brought her home. She's been mad at me ever since, because it made her face the fact that she needs help." She turned to Mike and asked teasingly, "Or is cussedness a quality I might have gotten from you?"

"Absolutely not," Mike replied with a straight face.

Brandon could see it in the rearview mirror. "What?" he challenged.

"All right, maybe sometimes," Mike conceded. "Is anybody else ready for lunch?" They were on the outskirts of Sacramento.

Angie smiled at his obvious ploy to change the subject and quickly agreed that it was time for a break.

WHEN THEY GOT BACK into the car, Brandon took the driver's seat as he'd predicted and Angie climbed into the back.

She had a perfect view of the back of Brandon's head, and stared unabashedly at his neatly barbered hair. It was very dark against the neckline of the white sweatshirt. His neck and shoulders looked as though they'd either seen ambitious yard work or spent time with weights.

He turned the car onto the interstate, and for the next hour, traffic was so dense that no one spoke.

Congestion began to diminish farther south, and Brandon put a CD in the disk player. Angie was shocked when George Strait's voice crooned through the speakers.

"You like George Strait?" she asked in disbelief.

Brandon found her gaze in the rearview mirror. "No!" he denied in amused vehemence. "But your mother told Mike you did, so he bought the disk yesterday. My pleas for a new Wynton Marsalis tape were ignored, thank you very much."

Angie laughed. "Well, George is better for a mellow mood anyway. After fighting that traffic, I'd need a long bath and a bottle of Bordeaux."

He frowned at her in the mirror. "You're telling me there was no traffic in New York?" He turned the volume down on the CD player as he awaited her answer.

"I didn't drive in New York," she replied. "I took the subway."

He frowned. "Then you'd need a bath, a bottle and a bodyguard."

She had to laugh. "I, mercifully, never had any trouble."

Mike launched into the praises of Los Angeles over other big cities, and Angie was reminded of her mother's concern that Mike would try to coax her to stay.

He finished with, "And the weather's definitely better than New York."

Brandon turned the volume up again and they spent the rest of the afternoon listening to music. They stopped once for gas and freshening up, then pulled into an Italian restaurant for dinner in Bakersfield.

"Another three hours or so, and we'll have you home," Mike said to Angie as the waiter cleared away their dishes. "You feeling tired?"

"No, I'm fine. You two have done all the work."

"Well, rest up," Mike said, putting his hand over hers on the table. "Because we'll give you one day to settle in, then Brandon's going to work on you."

Brandon raised an eyebrow.

Angie noted that and felt her own concern. He was, obviously, aware of the curious connection they had—whatever it was.

Brandon sipped at his coffee. "Me?" he asked calmly as he put the cup down.

"You," Mike confirmed. "I was thinking about it this afternoon. I know the plan was to have Betsy handle getting Angie ready for the camera, but I'd really rather you did. You're the marketing genius—you've got the fairy-tale hook locked in—you date women who wear dynamite clothes. You know exactly what we're trying to do here."

"But the launch of Daratin is..."

"I'll handle antihistamines. You take care of Rapunzel and get to know your sister."

"My sister."

Angie heard the ironic tone in Brandon's voice and knew it clearly meant he didn't want her as a sister. She just wasn't sure why. He'd assured her that he wasn't interested in Mike's money, and she was inclined to believe him. Besides, if he was the hotshot Mike claimed he was, he was probably making enough on his own.

But it was entirely possible that the man whose parents had so neglected him didn't care to share his foster father's love and attention with anyone—particularly a daughter Mike hadn't even known about, who'd come into his life on the strangest of flukes. Perhaps Brandon was willing to tolerate her for the time it would take to put together the hair-care products campaign, but he wasn't interested in a long-term connection—despite their attraction.

Mike turned to her, apparently unaware of any ambivalence between her and Brandon. "Though Brandon never let me formally adopt him, he's been more of a son to me than any child who could have come from my seed. It's important to me that you understand that."

She had no idea what the men had been through

together in the almost twenty years since Brandon had become part of Mike's life, but the depth of Mike's sincerity was bright in his eyes.

"And that you behave accordingly," Brandon put in, apparently hoping to lighten the emotional moment. "We have to establish now that I'm the favorite, Sis."

She had to banish the small, but present, tension between the foster son and the natural daughter once and for all.

"That's fine, brother o' mine, as long as we make sure that I'm the spoiled one." She smiled winningly at Mike. "May I have dessert, please?"

Mike laughed at her audacity and grinned at Brandon. "She's going to keep you on your toes." He signaled for the waiter.

Brandon rolled his eyes. "Why couldn't you have had a son? I could have used a hand with the lawn mowing."

"I happen to be excellent at lawn mowing," Angie retorted, then said to the waiter, who'd returned with a questioning look, "The mousse I saw you deliver to that table—was that chocolate?"

"Coffee and rum, signorina," he replied.

"Wonderful. I'd like one, please."

"Of course. Anyone else?"

"I'll have one," Mike said. "Brandon?"

"You're supposed to watch your intake of—" Brandon began, but Mike cut him off.

"Bring three, please," he said to the waiter.

Brandon frowned across the table at Angie. "It's taken me two months to wean him off desserts since his heart attack. If you're going to be a bad influence, I pass on to you the duty of nagging him about it.''

"Oh," she said in apologetic concern. "I'm sorry. I wasn't thinking."

Mike glowered at Brandon, who met the look without flinching. "My heart attack wasn't that serious, but I am supposed to watch my diet and get some exercise so that it doesn't happen again. But a little mousse won't hurt me."

"That's what you said about the little banana split and the little German chocolate cake when we drove up to the lake."

"I know just how to handle this," Angie said with a wink in Mike's direction.

"How?" Brandon asked warily.

"When his dessert comes, you and I will share it," she said, pleased with herself. She smiled modestly, picked up her coffee cup and gave Brandon a teasingly superior look over its rim. "I guess I'm the smart one, too, aren't I?"

Chapter Six

Angie was asleep in the front seat beside Brandon when he turned into Mike's box-hedge-lined driveway. Brandon pulled into the four-car garage that was also occupied by his red Firebird convertible and Mike's classic Daimler and Bugatti.

The sensor light went on, bathing the room in glaring light.

Mike climbed out of the back, opened the passenger door and leaned in to wake Angie.

Brandon took the bags out of the trunk and carried them into the kitchen. The spotless glass and brick gleamed in the low light Dunston had left on for their late arrival. It was good to be home, he thought, though the lake had certainly been more interesting this visit than he usually found it.

He turned toward the door to the garage, expecting to find Mike and Angie behind him. But they weren't, and the garage was silent.

He went back to the car to see what was keeping them, and found Mike still trying to wake his sleeping daughter. He straightened with a grin when he heard Brandon.

"I'm getting nowhere," he said. "Gretta was just like that—dozed off in an instant and slept like a rock. You think you can get her upstairs?"

"Sure." The last time he'd had an armful of Angie Corwin, she'd left an emotional and a physical impression he could still feel. But he didn't want Mike to know he had lascivious thoughts about his daughter, so he leaned down and scooped her out of the car with a clinical detachment he thought appeared genuine.

Angie stirred, made a little sound of protest without opening her eyes, then looped her arms around his neck and leaned into him.

Mike closed the car door, then hurried ahead of him, clearing his path, opening doors.

Brandon climbed the wide, mahogany-spindled staircase, then followed Mike down the beige-carpeted hall to the room that overlooked the garden. As he walked, he felt Angie's braid bump against his arm.

Mike went into the dark, cool room to flip on the small Tiffany lamp on the bedside table.

Brandon followed and stood at the side of the bed with Angie while Mike tossed the covers back.

"Hold on," Mike said, hurrying around to the other side of the bed. "The sheet's stuck. I swear, Dunston makes beds like there's a sergeant around who's going to bounce a quarter off of them."

All of a sudden, Angie awoke. He felt her little start of surprise and confusion as she looked around. He opened his mouth to reassure her, but when her eyes fell on him, he knew no words were necessary.

He felt the difference in her immediately, the dissipation of tension, the relaxation of her body back into the cradle of his arms.

But her eyes remained on him, and every coil of tension that left her now invaded him. Her eyes were going over his face, feature by feature, almost as though she'd never seen him before.

Then Mike said from across the bed, "Got it. You can put her down now."

Brandon leaned down to deposit her on the closest side of the downy mattress covered in ivy-patterned sheets. He placed her head on the soft pillow and straightened.

But the fractured, colored light from the lamp made her look as though she were an angel in a church window, and he didn't seem to be able to stop staring.

Then Mike came around the bed and she quickly lowered her eyelids.

"I'll get her bags," Brandon said, eager to have an excuse to leave the room.

Angie didn't watch him go because she didn't want Mike to know something was brewing here. She didn't really like knowing it herself. It added a thread of complexity to a situation that was already difficult.

"Sorry," Angie said to Mike as she sat up sleepily in the bed. "I guess I wasn't much company coming through L.A. I'm sorry. I wanted to see it, too."

"You'll have ample opportunity to see it over the next week." Mike pointed to a door behind him. "Bathroom's in there." Then he gestured toward a pair of louvered doors across the room. "Closet's over there." He went on to point out a half door behind a soft green, balloon-back chair. "And there's a dumbwaiter, if you ever don't feel like coming down for meals.''

She blinked at him. "You're kidding. You really have one of those?" Then she looked around herself and realized by the vast proportions of the room and the height of the ceilings that the house must be very large.

"Yes, we do." Mike sat on the edge of the bed, obviously pleased to be in possession of something that fascinated her. "And we have a revolving buffet between the living room and dining room, an art-nouveau ceramic fireplace, a Shakespeare garden and a gardener's cottage. This place was built in the twenties by Reginald Lyle.''

Angie looked around again, even more astonished. "The silent film star," she said with reverence, imagining that some bygone diva of the soundstage had probably slept in this bed. If it was, in fact, even called a soundstage when there was no sound.

"Yes. He was rather flamboyant, I guess, and threw weekend parties that involved scores of people.''

"I wonder what they ate," she asked seriously.

Mike laughed. "That, I don't know. Anything I can get you before you settle down for the night?"

"Just my bags.''

"Here they are." Brandon appeared in the doorway with them. "By the closet or by the bed?" he asked.

She pointed to the closet doors just a few steps from where he stood. She preferred he didn't come any closer at the moment. "Right there. Thank you.''

He placed the bags in front of the closet doors, then slipped the strap of a leather purse off his shoulder and came close enough to lob it by its strap to the foot of the bed. "Sleep well," he said. "I'll be gone by—"

"No, you won't," Mike interrupted. "I'd like you to take her around tomorrow—wherever she wants to go."

Brandon looked as though he wanted to argue, but he said simply, "I thought you'd want to do that."

Mike sighed. "I do. But I'm feeling kind of..."

"What?" Brandon's question was swift, concerned.

"Tired. I thought I'd just rest up tomorrow."

"I don't have to go anywhere," Angie said amiably. "I'll be happy to just stay—"

"Nonsense," Mike interrupted once more. "I want you to have some fun, maybe see some theater."

"Isn't part of the reason I'm here for us to get to know each other?"

"We'll have lots of time for that. I don't want you hanging around an empty house with nothing to do."

"I could cook for you," Angie said brightly, desperately.

Mike smiled. "Dunston does that. You'll meet him at breakfast. He's a great butler, marvelous cook and a good friend. You get comfortable now, and if you need anything, I'm at the end of the hall and Brandon's just opposite you. There's also an intercom in every room. The green button's for Dunston if you get hungry or need more towels or blankets."

Out of arguments, Angie glanced at Brandon, who appeared perfectly calm, except that they had some sensory connection she couldn't explain, and she knew he was as reluctant to spend a day alone with her, as she was to spend it with him.

But neither of them wanted to upset Mike. It was becoming rapidly clear that that was going to become the big problem here.

"See you at breakfast," he said with a fraternal smile, and turned to leave Mike to say good-night.

"Good night, Brandon," Mike said from the edge of Angie's bed. He faced her, his expression suddenly grave. "You understand that I'm not trying to...to *buy* your affection, or come on like a cozy parent, when I didn't even know you existed three days ago. But now that you're in my world—part of Gretta, part of me— the flower of that mountain summer..." He looked overwhelmed suddenly, and Angie put a hand on his arm.

"I...find myself wanting to give you things, show you off," he said with a self-deprecating laugh.

She laughed, too, thinking that she liked that vulnerability in him. She liked *him*—a lot. "I don't want anything," she said. "But I guess you can show me off sometime if you want to."

"Good." He gave her a hug, then stood and went to the door. He turned at the threshold. "You sure your mother will be all right all alone?"

"I'm sure," she replied. "Becky Flynn, my assistant at the shop, will be staying with her at night and preparing breakfast and dinner. I left frozen lunches for her."

"But she'll miss you. You'll miss her."

Angie shrugged a shoulder. "That's a sad fact of our lives, I'm afraid. We've spent a lot of time apart."

He frowned over that. "I should have suspected that a child had come from that summer. It was so...

explosive, so...deep. I should have gone to Tanzania to see her. Then I'd have learned the truth."

"She should have told you the truth. It is the way it is and we can't change it." Angie got to her feet and went to the door. "I'm just happy to have found you now. I want you to be happy, too. Not to recriminate or regret."

He took her in his arms and crushed her to him, fatherly strength and security in his embrace. "How could I regret anything that resulted in you?" he whispered heavily.

Then he straightened and ran a hand over the hair at the crown of her head, his eyes dark with emotion. "Good night, Angie."

"Good night, Dad," she said.

BRANDON, WEARING fleece shorts to sleep in, in deference to Angie's presence in the house, rapped on Mike's bedroom door. When there was no answer, he pushed his way in, certain something must be wrong. The whole eventful trip had been too much for him. He'd known it.

He found Mike in the dark in his big chair, a snifter of brandy in his hand. He was staring at nothing.

Brandon flipped the light on and leaned over his chair, bracing himself to find him comatose—or worse.

But Mike's bright-eyed gaze was healthy except for the tears glistening there. And as he turned his head to look at him, Brandon saw that he was smiling.

Brandon eased to one knee beside his chair. "You all right?" he asked.

Mike's bottom lip quivered, then his voice came out in a low rasp. "She called me 'Dad.'"

"ANGIE, JUST TELL ME where you want to go."

"I don't know where I want to go, Brandon. I've never been here before."

"Beach, museums, shopping—what?"

"Wherever you'd like to go."

"I'd like to go to work. The question is, where would *you* like to go?"

Brandon wasn't wild about conducting an argument while fighting the midmorning traffic on the 405 freeway. He preferred to give one or the other his complete attention.

He and Angie had eaten breakfast with Mike in companionable conversation while Dunston served, cautious at first, then obviously smitten with the new arrival. By the time Mike had run through all their plans for the campaign with Angie and Dunston had made her another of his famous sweet-cream waffles, discussed the details of its ingredients with her and flushed nauseatingly under her praise, it was after eleven.

"I know you don't want to do this any more than I do." Angie's left hand came into his field of vision as she gestured emphatically. "So, why don't you just drop me somewhere and come back for me at dinnertime. We'll make up a story to tell my father about where we went."

"Lying to Mike," Brandon said reproachfully. "That's a great way for you to begin a relationship."

She growled. "How would punching you in the nose be for beginning ours?" she demanded.

"Fatal for you," he replied quietly. "Trust me on that."

To his exasperation, she made a disbelieving sound. "Yeah, right. Like you have a violent bone in your body." She laid her head against the rest with an angry movement. "I'm trying to find a solution to the problem of being in each other's company."

"There isn't one." Mike passed a pickup with an unsteady load and slipped into the slow lane. If she insisted on arguing, he wasn't going to do his part while going eighty. "We're facing a week of having to pretend that we have platonic feelings for each other."

He felt, rather than saw, Angie turn toward him. In the slow lane, he had time to glance at her and challenge her to deny what he suggested.

She didn't. She simply looked back at him, those jade eyes wide and mystified. She'd tied her hair into a high ponytail this morning. It hung over her shoulder, a dark-red hank of silk in which light moved.

"I don't understand it," she said, her tone quiet but mildly defensive. "We barely know each other. It doesn't make sense."

He looked back at the road again. "The same standards don't apply to sense and sex."

She was quiet for a moment. He felt a sudden and desperate need for speed, but knew he didn't have the focus to control it. He continued to keep his place between the old Volkswagen bug in front of him and the beater station wagon behind him.

"Sex?" she asked. There was a suggestion of indignation in her voice, and a little edge of disappointment. "What I feel for you has nothing to do with *sex.*"

He glanced at her quickly, then back at the road again. Her eyes magnetized something soft inside him and tried to pull it up. He fought it.

"We feel attraction," he said. "Same thing."

"I beg to differ with you, but it's not." He heard her huff impatiently. "Sex is physical, spontaneous, elemental. What I feel is..."

He risked another glance at her. She was staring moodily at him, obviously thinking. He waited.

She finally sighed and straightened in her seat. But she said nothing.

"You feel what?" he asked.

"If what *you* feel is sexual," she said a little stiffly, "I think I'll keep what I feel to myself."

He was surprised to find that he was enormously disappointed. But he had to remember that at heart he stood alone in the world—except for Mike.

"It's only been a few days," he grumbled. "And you'll only be here a week. That's too short a time for...anything."

She expelled a breath and settled more comfortably in her seat. "You would think so, but that doesn't seem to be the case, does it? Well, let's just forget it."

"Good," he said. "Now maybe we can decide where you'd like to go."

There was a moment's silence, then she said, "Disneyland."

"Disneyland?"

"I AM NOT riding on a teacup," Brandon said forcefully. "And that is final. But I'll be happy to wait for you."

Angie had made a decision. It didn't matter that the lofty feelings that motivated her attraction to Brandon didn't match the elementary feelings that motivated his for her.

It didn't matter that his interest in her was... whatever it was. Actually, it did matter a little. It was exciting that he found her sexually attractive. But it wasn't enough to make it worthy of exploration.

She'd spent her whole life wanting all the things she'd been lonely for as a child—affection, attention, indulgence, security, stability. She wasn't going to be distracted from a search for it by a man to whom she was simply a responding set of hormones.

But it did matter that he was her father's foster son. She and Brandon faced something of a future together—however intermittent their meetings might be. It was important that they be friends.

"Well, what *will* you ride on?" she asked, in an effort to be conciliatory.

"Why do I have to ride on anything?"

"Because you promised to show me a good time. I've spent most of my life having to entertain myself. Now that I have a brother, so to speak, I think you should have to go on rides with me."

He took her arm and led her away from the teacups. "You are about to learn the dangers of harassing an older sibling."

"Really." She let herself be led along, pretending

not to be concerned. "You don't scare me. I happen to know the crocodiles in Adventureland are robots."

By the time he'd finished with her, *she* was feeling distinctly robotic. He pulled her into a bobsled on the Matterhorn, and then onto the rope bridge on Tom Sawyer Island, with a group of rowdy teenagers in front of them and behind them. He took her through the Indiana Jones Adventure, where a jeep on rails raced them through snakes, rats, mummies and just ahead of a giant rolling ball of granite—and then on every other dark and scary speed ride in the park.

She was windblown, sunburned and frazzled when they were finished. And she was sure she was moving like something without joints. But she'd never had such a great time in her life.

Brandon, pulling her down beside him onto a bench in the area called Old New Orleans, looked with puzzled amusement into her laughing face. Strands of her ponytail had whipped over her head during the last turn on Mr. Toad's Wild Ride, and he smoothed them back in place.

"I was hoping you'd be sick by now," he said. "This won't be half as much fun for me if you *like* it."

"Sorry." She put a hand to her pounding heart. "I have a cast-iron stomach. Always have had. I ate grubs and beetles with the Masai kids."

He winced. "I'm delighted to know that."

"And I've only been to one other amusement park in my life."

"You're kidding."

She was surprised that he thought so. "They didn't

have any where Mom was in Africa, and I was always too busy as an adult. But when I graduated from boarding school, the teachers took us to one. I had the best time. I never forgot it. And this…'' She raised both arms, then let them fall to indicate there was no describing what she felt. "I don't know. I hate the thought of leaving. I wish we could do the shoot here.''

Brandon knew he was going to hate himself for this. He shouldn't even suggest it. But despite the argument in the car and his recalcitrant behavior when they'd first arrived, she'd behaved without rancor. And when he'd taken her on every stomach-churning, breath-stealing ride as a sort of punishment for making him *want* to know how she felt about him, she'd been a good sport. Even he'd had a good time.

"You want to stay for dinner and watch the fireworks?'' he asked.

Her eyes lit up. "Fireworks?'' Then her expression became reluctant. "But Mike's expecting us for dinner, isn't he?''

"I don't think he'd mind if you're having a good time. I'll find a phone and let him know.''

She caught his arm when he tried to stand. "But do *you* want to stay?''

"Sure.''

"Just to humor me, or because you're having a good time, too?''

"Because I haven't finished with you yet,'' he threatened with a grin. "Let's see how sassy you are on the rocket jets after dinner and dessert.''

She laughed. ''In that case, call him. Tell him I said hi.''

BRANDON TOOK Angie to the dining show at Aladdin's Oasis, where the meal was so superb she pleaded with him to change his mind about the rocket jets.

''All right,'' he said, teasingly reluctant. ''Since you were such a good dinner companion. But what do you want to do until it's dark enough for fireworks?''

''Wander up and down Main Street?'' she suggested, rubbing her arms against the cooling temperature of evening.

''Didn't you bring a sweater?'' he asked.

''I left it in the car.'' she replied. ''It was so warm, and I didn't expect to be out in the evening.'' She pointed to his bare arms. ''Where's *your* sweater?''

He grinned. ''Also in the car.''

''If you stay here and wait for me,'' she said, ''I'll run to the car for them.''

He laughed lightly. ''You remember where we're parked?''

''Um…'' She pointed. ''That way.''

He rolled his eyes. ''Angie, there are thousands of cars in the lot. I have a better idea.''

''What?''

He caught her hand and pulled her after him. He led her into a clothing shop filled with garments bearing images of the Disney characters, from a subtle inch-square picture on a pocket, to a face that covered an entire shirtfront.

He held up a denim jacket with an embroidered image of Mickey Mouse on the back. "How's this?" he asked.

"Great, but..." She moved toward him to him to check the price tag.

"My gift to you," he said. He held it open for her to try on.

"No," she said emphatically, slipping her arms into the sleeves. "I never accept gifts from men."

"You're the one who said I was supposed to show you a good time," he said, pushing her toward a three-way mirror. "That includes preventing you from catching cold."

She studied her reflection. The jacket fitted perfectly and gave her silky blue-flowered dress a funky look. She turned to admire the image on the back and watched it repeat itself endlessly through the reflecting mirrors.

"May I help you?" a young woman in a Donald Duck sweatshirt asked. A badge identified her as a clerk.

Brandon handed her a credit card. "We'll take the jacket. She'd like to wear it."

Angie reached down for her purse at the same moment that the woman took a pair of scissors out of her pocket. She snipped off the tag and went away with Brandon's card.

"But I..." Angie called after her. It was too late. She turned to Brandon, her expression displeased.

"Relax," he said, lowering his voice. "It's not like I'm going to demand 'payment' for it."

She gave him a look of bland disbelief. "How do I

know that?'' she whispered back. ''All you feel for me is sexual.''

He closed his eyes to summon patience. When he opened them again, she was standing in front of the mirror, trying on a baseball cap. It wouldn't fit over her ponytail. She took the clip off and combed her fingers through her hair until it lay about her back and shoulders like a veil of dark fire.

He'd been about to refute her statement, but he couldn't look at that glorious hair without wondering what it would feel like draped over him in the throes of lovemaking.

''I didn't say that was *all* I felt, did I?'' he asked.

She caught his eye in the mirror, and her hand stopped in the act of adjusting the cap's visor. Her eyes were big, startled.

And that was as close as he was getting to that right now. ''I'll meet you at the counter,'' he said.

Angie watched him walk away and felt excitement and self-deprecation at the same time. The reason for her excitement was obvious; he felt something for her that was more than physical. She liked that.

But she also saw the danger it presented. *He* didn't like that he felt that, and that would be trouble. She imagined she could allow him to be reluctant to care, considering his childhood and the self-protective tricks he must have had to learn simply to remain sane.

The question in the long run, though, was what would that mean as far as she was concerned?

She comforted herself with the decision that it was futile to worry about it. Tomorrow she would begin work on her father's ad campaign, and though he'd put Brandon in charge of it, they would be spending far less time alone together. And as he'd pointed out earlier, she would be gone in a week.

Maybe her interest would pale. Maybe his would.

In the meantime, she found a good way to pay him back for what he'd put her through on the rides this afternoon and for insisting on buying the jacket.

She peered around his arm as he signed the credit card transmittal at the counter. "I'm running into the ladies' room. I'll meet you in front of the store."

"Sure."

The sky was darkening when she came out of the shop. He straightened away from a pole against which he'd been leaning and admired the fit of the jacket on her. Maybe a funky look would also be good for the younger market in the Rapunzel campaign. He'd have to run it by Mike.

She held a sack out to him. "Something for you," she said.

He looked at it suspiciously.

She shook her head at him and unrolled the top of the bag. "Turn around," she directed, pulling something out of the sack.

"Why?" he asked.

She cocked her head impatiently. "So I can knock you unconscious and steal all your money. Just turn around."

He did, and then felt her take his right arm. Something slid over it. When she did the same thing with his left, he realized he was being fitted into a shirt...no...a jacket.

He turned to her, holding out the sleeves of the

denim jacket he wore. He put his hands on his hips and scolded her with a look.

"Why did you do that?"

She shrugged innocently. "Because it was so you."

"Mickey is so me?" he asked doubtfully.

She pulled him toward the store window, having difficulty biting back a laugh. She turned him so that he could see his back reflected. He wore the image of Winnie the Pooh's friend Tigger.

He studied her with a puzzled look. "So me?"

She grinned. "Yes. A tiger that's sweet rather than scary."

He winced. "Sweet?"

She nodded apologetically. "I'm sorry, but you are. I know that you don't want to be, but you are."

The moment was electric. She saw the power surge in his eyes as they settled on her lips, felt the systems stall in her spine. He was going to kiss her.

Their mouths were so close together the kiss was a fact before she'd finished the thought. It began assertively, without roughness but without the gentleness that usually defined him.

He was trying to make a point, she guessed. She tried to imagine what he must be thinking. *This is how it will be with me, because this is how I feel. This is purely sexual. That's all.*

But he didn't know himself very well. His hands made a different statement entirely. One was splayed in the middle of her back, holding her tenderly, protectively. The other cupped her chin between his thumb and forefinger, the hold gentle, the thumb tracing a caress along the line of her throat.

She threaded her fingers into his thick, wiry hair and responded to his mobile lips with her own message. She leaned into him trustingly, and when he freed her chin to run a hand over her hair, she framed his face in her hands and looked into his eyes, wordlessly telling him, *This is how it will be with me. Sexual, certainly, but born of a powerful attraction to a masculinity that is tough and strong but seems always to be used with kindness, an attraction that is quickly, deeply, apparently irretrievably, giving life to something else. It's something too new to name, but undeniably there—and it doesn't matter a damn that we've only known each other four days.*

And then she stood on tiptoe and opened her mouth over his.

Brandon felt a part of him trying to pull away, trying to resist the insidiously warm lips on his that were slowing and prolonging the kiss. He'd wanted it to be pleasurable but emphatic.

Yet another part of him was happily enslaved by her small hands tracing his jaw, shaping his cheekbones, delving into his hair. Her mouth was gentle but generous, probing his for a response he forgot for a moment he was determined to withhold.

The moment he felt trust begin to surface, he took a fistful of her hair and reclaimed control of the encounter. He kissed her soundly, deeply, then raised his head and looked into her eyes.

At the same moment, there was a rumbling explosion behind him and he saw fireworks reflected in Angie's gaze.

Chapter Seven

Brandon pulled the Firebird up in front of an exclusive little salon on a side street off Rodeo Drive. Angie sat quietly beside him, a little less animated than usual. But he could understand that.

After last night, he was not himself, either. He didn't know who he was. And he didn't like the feeling at all. Not even in the darkest moments of his life on the street had he lost the sense of who he was and what he wanted to do.

Now that seemed clouded by the inescapable pervasiveness of the memory of a kiss. It had lived with him while he and Angie stood companionably side by side last night and watched the fireworks, persisted on the quiet drive home and for every moment of the long, long night.

This morning, he and Angie had greeted each other cheerfully across the breakfast table for Mike's benefit, but Brandon had seen her glance bounce off him more than once when he'd turned to catch her watching him.

She didn't look as though she'd been troubled by lack of sleep. He didn't like that. She probably thought that kiss had sealed his fate. That she'd made him see that his feelings ran deeper than lust.

She'd piled her hair on top of her head today in a complicated coil. She was wearing a yellow skirt and top and high-heeled shoes. She reminded him of a candle—a very beautiful candle.

He came around the car to help her out. The height of her heels raised the top of her head to his eyes rather than his nose, and when she straightened out of the car and looked him in the eye, he felt challenged.

Then she smiled, and any aggressive reaction he might have experienced dissipated before it could take shape.

She looked up at the bright blue sky, then at the fashionable but lightly garbed pedestrians moving along the street and shook her head. "How do you get used to it being summer all the time? I mean, it's wonderful, for a while. But it's like this year-round?"

He took her arm and pulled her with him up the short, flower-lined walkway. "Mostly. Every once in a while we get a cold snap and the weather gets down into the fifties."

She stopped as he reached around her to open the door. "Don't you miss autumn leaves? Snow?"

He considered that. "I can go to Gray Goose Lake for that. But I lived on the street long enough to be grateful for a warm climate. Every time it rains, I think about the people I was with and wonder if they've found an open basement or a dry doorway."

Her eyes softened, but it wasn't pity he saw there; it was sadness, caring. "I'm sorry that happened to you," she said gently.

He wanted to kiss her again, but he'd decided at about three this morning that he was not going down that road. "I survived," he replied.

The look in her eyes changed subtly to one of indulgent disbelief.

He knew what it suggested. That he'd survived, all right, but not without some emotional damage. He opened his mouth to challenge her on that score, when the door shot open and Emilio Gutierrez appeared in the opening.

"Hey, gringo, you're crowding my doorway." The lightly accented criticism was accompanied by the contradiction of a wide smile and a hand extended in friendship. "How you been, Brandon?"

"Good." Brandon shook Emilio's hand and introduced him to Angie. "Emilio and I shared the downtown paper route when we were kids."

Angie extended her hand to the handsome Latino. He was half a head shorter than Brandon, muscularly built in a crisp white shirt and black jeans. Slightly sloe-eyed, exaggerated by prominent cheekbones and a very white smile that he used generously, he was devilishly good-looking.

"Then he went to fat city," Emilio said with a thumb jabbed in his friend's direction, "and I went to Juvie. Where's the justice?"

Despite the words, Emilio's swing at Brandon's shoulder suggested friendship rather than resentment.

"And now limos and personal jets pick you up and take you to celebrities' homes so you can do their hair," Brandon said dryly, "while I live my life in an office. You tell *me* where the justice is."

"You're heir to a Fortune 500 company."

"You've built an empire on your own."

"Would it make either of you feel better," Angie interposed, looking from one to the other, "to know that all I have is a tea shop in the wilds of northern California?"

The men laughed, then Emilio caught Angie's arm and pulled her into the shop. "Let's see that hair, chica. It looks as though it's all you need in this world."

He led her into a vast blue-and-silver shop, where the strains of a Serena tune mingled with the windy whir of blow dryers.

There were several dozen stations comprised of chair, sink, countertop and drawers. Walls of mirror reflected bushy hanging ferns, tall, standing palms, and blue-smocked hairdressers of various sizes and descriptions shampooing, drying, cutting and curling.

Under their nimble fingers were the trusting heads of blondes, brunettes, redheads, and several graying matrons. Many of them turned at the unusual sight of a male customer in the shop.

Angie was surprised when Brandon seemed to take their attention in stride and return their interested looks with a smile as Emilio led the way to the back of the shop.

"You going to stay and criticize?" Emilio asked Brandon as he helped Angie into a plump, blue shop chair.

Brandon leaned a hip on the counter and folded his arms. "Absolutely. I don't want you to get scissor crazy here."

Emilio pulled the pins out of Angie's hair. "I thought you came here because you trust me to do a good job for you."

"Yeah, well, I trust you better when I can watch you."

Emilio smiled into the mirror at Angie. "He has unresolved trust issues."

Angie smiled back. "I've noticed that."

"Madre de Dios!" The exclamation came from Emilio as Angie's dark red hair, finally free of confinement, fell past the back of the chair and well below it. He combed his fingers through it, holding one long skein out from her head and letting it fall back slowly. "It's like a rain of fire," he said with the reverence of a connoisseur. Then he added something in Spanish, which Angie couldn't understand.

She glanced at Brandon.

"Something about wanting to kidnap you, I think," he translated with a grin.

Emilio placed both hands on Angie's head and met her eyes in the mirror, his own theatrically grave. "Seriously, amigo. I give you my entire fortune for this woman."

Angie rolled her eyes at the man's exaggeration.

Brandon made a thoughtful face. "Specify *entire*," he said.

"Everything." Emilio made a grand gesture with both arms. "My shops, my condo in Aspen, my holdings in Planet Hollywood, my plane."

"What about the Mark 8 Jag?"

"Man, we'll need something to get around in."

"Ah…hello?" Angie raised both hands. Emilio and

Brandon gave her their attention. "Besides the fact that Brandon isn't empowered to negotiate for me," she said, aiming a dark glance at him in the mirror, then one at Emilio, "if you give away your fortune, how do you intend to support me?"

Emilio frowned back, a smile barely suppressed. "I thought you had a tearoom in the wilds of California?"

"You want to kidnap me so that I can support *you?*"

"*Sí.* Isn't it romantic?"

"I think I'll say no, thank you."

"You want to stay with Brandon? But he has trust issues."

"I am not *with* Brandon," Angie corrected mildly. "And you, *señor,* have delirium issues."

Brandon moved to stand behind the chair while Emilio went to work. He watched him shampoo her hair, towel it, then comb it back.

"Don't look at my freckles," she implored of Brandon's reflection. She wore a plastic cape like some slightly backward superheroine.

"Hard not to," he said, laughing lightly. "They're all over the place."

"You're sure I'm right for this?"

"I'm sure."

"Okay." Emilio took the ends of a section of hair between his first two fingers and held it up to Brandon, who leaned over attentively. "Her hair is in wonderful condition, but always, with very long hair, there are split ends. I can just trim the bottom to get rid of those. But if you want—" he waved one hand still holding scissors and comb "—movement…I have to cut a couple of inches."

"How many?"

Emilio freed the hair, combed it down, then held the side of his hand about three inches up from the tips. "About here. Dry, it will come to her shoulder blades."

Brandon met Angie's eyes in the mirror. "Can you live with that?"

Emilio looked up to await her answer.

"Yes," she replied. "Sure."

"Okay." Emilio put his hands to the sides of her face and pulled some of the damp hair forward. "If I angle the sides toward her face, she will look absolutely *delicioso*."

Brandon looked doubtful. "You mean more cutting?"

"Yes. A little."

"What do you think, Angie?"

"Emilio knows what he's doing."

"I do," Emilio said confidently. "It will not only frame her *cara linda*, but it will give her hair all the movement you wish to prove your shampoo provides. And the back will still be long and thick so that you can do that shot for TV where the hair tumbles down."

Brandon's reflection raised a questioning eyebrow at Angie's.

She smiled at Emilio's image in the mirror.

"*I* do not have trust issues. Do it."

Emilio pushed Brandon toward a small canopied bar at the other end of the room, where an attendant made coffee drinks or poured cold drinks. "Have an espresso. I'll call you when I'm finished cutting. I don't want you to whine or faint.''

Brandon resisted his friend's effort to move him and pointed a warning finger at him. ''You blow this, *amigo,* and you won't have to worry about your shops, your condo, your shares in Planet Hollywood and your plane. I will personally put you back in that warehouse basement in the barrio.''

Emilio invoked the heavens with his eyes. ''Yada, yada, yada. I want you gone for twenty minutes.''

''All right. But remember that I can make you gone for a lifetime.''

As Brandon walked away with a look over his shoulder that left the impression he wasn't entirely kidding, Emilio set about giving Angie's hair another comb-through.

''Big guys,'' he said with a dramatic sigh. ''Always gotta threaten you. But that one's all talk.''

That made Angie wonder. ''Are you sure?''

He began to cut, starting with the hair at her sides, snipping it at an angle several inches below her chin. ''I'm sure,'' he said absently, concentrating on his work. ''When my old man died, and my mother took up with this drug dealer who hated my guts, I hit the street. But it was cold at night and rainy, and the shelters were scary, man.''

He combed again and snipped again, a little lower this time and still at an angle. ''I met Brandon when I tried to steal his bag of Doritos.'' Emilio laughed as he continued to cut. ''Man, he was on me like an army. Then, when he saw that I was hungry, he shared the bag with me and we became friends. He took me into this basement where he'd found a place to sleep.''

"And you've been friends ever since?"

Emilio straightened, turned her toward the mirror and studied his work. She saw that the hair on the right side of her face had been trimmed at a perfect angle to the very tips. She also saw that Emilio's expression had sobered and saddened. And she guessed it was the result of more than just the discussion about life on the street.

"Until I tried to frame him for a store I knocked over," he said, turning her so that he could work on the left side of her hair. "He lent me his jacket and I left it there in the back room so they'd think he did it."

She remembered his remark about going to Juvie. "But they didn't?"

He made a sound of self-deprecation. "Of course not. He's six inches taller than me, and they had me on the camera. Stupid. Stupid."

Angie didn't know what to say to that. She sat still as he worked and waited for him to go on.

"I went to Juvie, Mr. Rampion took Brandon in, and we didn't see each other till I got a job in construction while I was going to beauty school."

Angie smiled at the paradox of Emilio Gutierrez— a construction worker in beauty school.

"Brandon was twenty-two," Emilio went on. "Mike had settled some money on him, and Brandon was helping Father Saldana rebuild an old warehouse into a homeless shelter."

Angie sat up in surprise.

"Ay, *chica!* Don't move!" Emilio cautioned, then grinned. "If I blow this, you *will* have to support me with that tearoom."

"Sorry," she said. "So what happened."

"Well." Emilio combed and cut. "When I found out he was often around to check out the progress, I prayed we wouldn't meet. But I walked around a corner one day with a two-by-four and almost hit him. When he saw it was me, he asked me how I was and how I was doing."

"He wasn't…angry?"

"No. I, of course, had learned a lot since then and apologized all over the place, and he said he'd done a lot of things he wasn't proud of in those days, and it didn't matter anymore. Then he took me out for a beer."

Angie was silent. Then all she could manage was a quiet, "Wow."

"Yes," Emilio agreed. "Wow. He lent me the five thousand dollars that started my first shop ten years ago."

Angie let her eyes rove to what she could see of the room without moving her head. "Apparently, it was money well invested." Emilio straightened to study his work and she met his gaze in the mirror. "Maybe he has fewer trust issues than we think."

Emilio's smile was blindingly white. Then he tipped her head forward and began to work on the back of her hair. "I like to tease him about that because he dates only women whom he knows don't want to get serious, for one reason or another."

Angie stared at her lap. "So his trust issues are only with women?"

"I think, mostly, they're with himself. You know, having parents who don't care if you live or die, and living on the street, where you're just someone else for other people to step over, you pretty much lose all sense of value."

"But Mike considers him essential to the success of the business. He told me that Brandon has doubled sales since he's been in charge of marketing." In her vehemence, Angie forgot that she wasn't supposed to move. Emilio stopped and held scissors and comb safely away from her. "Because he targeted the market and managed to reach it."

Emilio nodded. "Yes. He is a business success. I am a business success. It's a matter of the farm and the girl."

"Pardon me?"

"You know that saying about taking the girl off the farm, but not getting…"

"The farm out of the girl. Yes. But how…"

"Because you can get a street rat out of the barrio, and he might learn to make his way, but at the heart of him, where he was most betrayed…" Emilio shrugged eloquently. "Well, that part heals more slowly. And because he's uncertain if there is love inside him—he can make love, but he has difficulty *giving* it."

"But he loves Mike."

He shook his head. "Love for another man doesn't require surrender, *chica*. Love for a woman does."

That explained, he turned her toward the mirror and tipped her head down again.

"Are you able to give love?" she asked, though she couldn't lift her head to see his response.

"Yes, but it took a long time. Fortunately, Juana was patient.

"Juana?"

He leaned around her chair to turn a two-fold picture frame toward her. On one side was a beautiful, dark-eyed woman in a prim and elegant white blouse, and on the other were a boy and a girl in a studio pose, the boy's arms wrapped around his younger sister. They looked happy and indulged.

"Juana took my loan application all those years ago," he said. He kissed his fingertips and applied them to her photo, then to that of the children. "Now I owe her my soul."

"So much for kidnapping me. Seems Brandon isn't the only who's all talk."

A TALL PEDESTAL glass appeared suddenly in front of Angie's face. It was filled with a cold, dark liquid and topped with a decorative mountain of whipped cream.

"An iced mocha!" she exclaimed, then looked into the mirror to see Brandon standing behind her. "Where's yours?"

"Drank it," he replied. "I'd have brought you one," he said to Emilio, "but I don't like you. How's it going?"

The gesture was thoughtful, but Angie was aware of feeling as pleased that Brandon was back as the fact that he'd brought her a drink. A few days ago she might have found that alarming. But today it was all too complex to even know what to be afraid of. So she just let it be.

"We're about to find out," Emilio said, stepping back to turn her this way and that while he checked out his work.

She sipped at her drink, needing the caffeine.

Emilio reached for a spray can. "Cellofix," he said, shaking it. "For volume." Angie noticed that the brand name on the can was Rampion.

Brandon took the mocha from Angie and put it safely out of the way while Emilio sprayed the substance over her wet head, then began to blow it dry.

Brandon, leaning against the counter to see her and not her reflection, noticed the transformation almost immediately. The angled sides curled toward each other with a suppleness that was everything Emilio had promised.

As his friend continued to move around Angie with the blow dryer, her hair began to gain volume and style. Then the color began to flame in it, and he felt a double-edged blade of excitement.

Professionally, he knew without a doubt that she was the perfect choice to sell Rapunzel. Her hair glistened like the sunset into which a man walked when his world had taken the perfect turn. It was his haven, his reward.

And an unexpected bonus of the hairstyle was that it gave her a more contemporary, stylish look so that the freshness and charm in her face shone vividly in contrast. It made her a fairy-tale heroine.

Personally, he felt as though the world, the planet,

was crowding him, pushing him toward her, closing off all means of escape. It didn't matter that he tried to back away; he was propelled inexorably toward her—and the closer he got, the more beautiful and seductive she became. He was ensnared. But he would fight it.

He tried to push aside what she was coming to mean to him and turned his concentration on what she meant to the Rapunzel campaign.

But he was watching her eyes as she studied her own reflection, and he saw them widen in pleased surprise. They'd looked like that last night when he'd kissed her to the thunder of fireworks.

He walked around the chair to study the back of her hair. Emilio had been right. It did look like raining fire.

"Lift it with your hands," Emilio suggested, "as though to get it off your neck, then let if fall slowly."

In the mirror, Brandon saw her raise her arms and fold them like some flightless angel, then lift the dark red veil of hair up. The flightless-angel metaphor that crossed his mind amused him, because the look her reflection gave him was pure Sadie Thompson. He could imagine her in a sarong in some seedy dive, undulating to the sound of drums. Vivid lust ignited in him.

Then she raised her hands higher, freeing her hair, and it tumbled down like a rumble of color, swinging, swaying, bouncing as it settled into place.

For an instant, he felt himself wrapped in it in some dark and silken place where they lay together in the aftermath of...

"Well!"

Emilio slapped him on the back with an enthusiasm that rattled his teeth.

"Tell me I'm not a genius!"

Brandon drew a deep breath to restore a sense of balance to his libido. He put an arm around Emilio's shoulders. "You're brilliant, *hombre*. That's why I brought her to you. Now I suppose I owe you *my* fortune."

Emilio focused on Angie's hair with an enimagtic smile. "No. I think I will give you this one because it will change everything." He studied Angie a moment longer, then turned to Brandon. "As your friendship changed things for me."

"Now, look..." Brandon began.

"End of discussion," Emilio said. He whipped the cape off Angie, brushed her off with a soft little broom and helped her up. "Now. Gloria Estefan's shooting a new video, and she's going to be here in five minutes. I have to make myself *hermoso* for her."

"You? Handsome?" Brandon shook his head as Emilio walked them to the door. "Shall I pray for a miracle?"

Emilio pulled the door open, hugged Angie as she walked through, then added quietly to Brandon, "You can afford to. You have *your* miracle."

"MAYBE I WON'T complain about perpetual summer anymore." They stood on the corner of Rodeo and Carmelita, waiting to cross the street. Angie spread her arms as though to call the sun to her. "The wonderful warmth is getting to me, seeping into my pores, making me feel lazy and languid.''

Brandon caught her hand to pull her with him as he crossed the street. "Well, forget that. You have a full day's work ahead of you."

She shielded her eyes against the sun as she hurried to keep up. "Doing what?"

"Trying on clothes. Buying shoes."

She put her wrist to her forehead, à la Blanche DuBois. "I'll try to be strong." They passed an elegant eatery as a trio of stylish women stepped into it. "Maybe it'd be easier," she said, trying to pull Brandon toward the door, "if I had some lunch."

He tugged against her and won. They walked on. "Robin said to bring you on an empty stomach."

"Who's Robin?" she asked. "And why would she persecute me like that?"

"Robin Atkins," he replied. "An up-and-coming young designer. She's doing your wardrobe for the shoot."

"Why do we need a wardrobe if you're going to photograph my *hair*?"

"Well, it would be nice if you were wearing something when we did it." He led her into an old but ornate office building.

"True," she admitted, "but the expense of..."

"We're talking national exposure, Angie," he explained patiently. "The expense is relatively minimal for Mike *and* it's a write-off. It'll also be good for Robin."

He tried to push her before him up a flight of stairs, but she resisted. Her expression was serious. "Mike doesn't think I'm doing this to get things, does he?''

"No."

"You're sure?"

"I'm sure."

She looked up the long, elegant High Gothic stairway. "We can lunch after the fitting?"

"From appetizers to dessert."

She started climbing.

Robin Atkins's studio took up half the top floor of the building and was a vast, open space except for the far end of it, which was walled off into an office, a changing room and a showroom of sorts.

A huge worktable stood in the middle of the floor and was surrounded by rolling racks of clothing on hangers, some items completed, some still pinned together. There were bolts and folds of fabric stored in cubbyholes against the wall, and racks, boxes and baskets of trim. Cones of thread hung from pegs on the wall, and the colorful array extended from floor to ceiling for several yards.

Two women worked at sewing machines by the window and didn't even look up when Brandon and Angie arrived.

But a brunette in black stirrups and a black T-shirt came out of the office, arms extended toward Brandon. He leaned down to embrace her.

The gesture was purely platonic, but Angie experienced a stab of jealousy anyway. Angie understood that it wasn't because Brandon had hugged another woman, but because she envied the comfortable ease with which they slipped into each other's arms.

Brandon looked around the room as Robin stepped back. "Where are the kids?"

"Getting flea-dipped," she replied.

At Angie's raised eyebrow, he explained with a laugh, "Her dogs. They're always here. Angie, Robin Atkins, brilliant designer. Robin, Angie Corwin, Rapunzel spokeswoman."

"Well." Robin stepped back to look her up and down, then nodded, as though she'd made some private decision. "I have a line that could have been made for her." Her eyes rose to Angie's hair. "That color is incredible. And Emilio did a wonderful job."

Angie ran a self-conscious hand over it. She found it a little strange to know she'd been discussed by everyone beforehand. That was necessary, of course, for this kind of project, but for a woman accustomed to the anonymity of the kitchen, it felt odd.

Brandon's eyes skimmed over her, settled on her lips for a moment, then went quickly back to Robin as though afraid to linger. "I was worried about cutting the sides, but Angie trusted him. Turns out she was right."

"Now you have to trust *me* to know what I'm doing," Robin said as she went to the edge of the room for a director's chair with her logo on it. "I want you to wait here while I show you what we can do with her. I've picked out some things that are already in the fitting room. You just be patient."

Brandon met her halfway and took the chair from her, placing it in the middle of the room. "Fine. I'll wait right here. And please *remember* that I'm waiting.

Don't turn this into one of those marathon 'getting-ready' things women do.''

Ignoring him, Robin hooked an arm in Angie's and walked her toward a paisley curtain near the office.

Chapter Eight

Angie came out of the dressing room in a roll-necked, white cat suit that clung to every lissome curve of her and made the breath catch in Brandon's throat.

"Lycra-silk," Robin said, stepping out from behind her, hands in the pockets of her pants. "Isn't it gorgeous? And the white's wonderful with her hair."

Brandon couldn't get his eyes up that high. They were skimming the soft, round contours of her breasts, the slight flare of hip, the length of thigh elongated by the single color and the tapering leg.

"Turn," Robin directed Angie.

Angie turned on her heel, arms slightly out for balance, and Brandon was reminded of a dove settling on a branch. For professional reasons—or so he told himself—he studied the way the stretchy fabric stretched across her "wings," clung to her waist, molded itself to the soft curve of her bottom. And then he forgot that he was being professional. He wanted to touch her, hold her, feel her roundness in the palms of his hands.

"What do you think?" Robin asked. "For that scene in front of the fireplace?"

Then he was forced to look up into Angie's face. The white *was* wonderful against her coloring. And with the tips of her hair turning inward and the rolled neck of the top concealing everything below her chin, her face resembled the heart of a flower. For a moment he couldn't look away...nor could he speak.

Angie had watched his eyes rove her body with bold, though respectful, interest and had been about to conclude that he didn't see her as anything other than a model in an ad campaign—a body connected to a particularly cooperative head of hair.

But now his eyes said something else entirely as he gazed into hers. He appeared startled, confused.

"I think," he said, his voice a little raspy and strained. He paused to clear his throat. "I think it's good. Good."

"Okay. On to the power suit."

Angie was pulled back behind the paisley curtain, where Robin helped her change into a white cotton shirt with pointed collar and French cuffs, a slim, tweedy brown skirt that stopped above her knee and a matching jacket.

Robin gave her large gold earrings and cuff links to match. Then she stood on a low stool and tied Angie's hair up in a loose knot.

"There," she said, stepping down again. "I'm not Emilio, but what do you think of the look?"

"I feel like a Wall Street mogul." Angie did a turn in the mirror. Her trimmed hair was less bulky when swept up and gave her a more delicate look. It occurred to her that that didn't fit entirely with the Wall Street look, but somehow it worked.

Brandon seemed to think so, too.

"Whoa," he said, his voice throaty.

"I feel as though I should sell you stocks or insurance," Angie said, doing the required turn in front of him. "And go to London with my commission."

"London?" he asked, his eyes going to her upswept hair. "Why not Barbados?"

"Because I couldn't wear this suit there," she replied, as though it should be obvious.

"Of course," he said, and gave Robin a thumbs-up. "Another keeper, Robin. What's next?"

"Cocktails," Robin replied. "Come on, Angie."

Brandon made it through the modeling of the cocktail dress, though it wasn't easy. The color was bright pink, the fabric georgette, according to Robin. Angie's shoulders were bare and wide straps came around her neck and looped into a diamond-shaped cutout just between and below her bosom. A rhinestone, chevron-shaped pin marked the bottom of the cutout.

Brandon's gaze went to it and was rewarded with just a glimpse of the round underside of a breast as she began the turn she now completed with accomplished grace. The skirt flared and so did his heartbeat.

But it was the negligee that did him in. It was black and simple and appeared to be silk. It clung to her, highlighting every plane and curve down to her ankles, with a wedge of fabric that allowed her to move. It rippled around her feet like the midnight surf.

Robin had loosened Angie's hair and it hung long and liquid as it had before, but the rearranging had mussed it, and she looked as though she'd just risen from some man's arms.

And that was the moment he understood the depth of what he felt for her. She was like a flame in his darkness. The arms from which she rose would have to be his from now on.

It didn't matter that he hadn't known of her existence a week ago. Fate could turn on a dime—lives changed in an instant; he'd already experienced that when Mike took him in.

"That's a definite," he said to Robin, but knew he was really telling himself.

He sat through several more changes, all charming, and Angie looked wonderful in all of them. But Robin had led with her personal favorites and—maybe he was learning something here—he trusted her to be right.

Angie invited Robin to join them for lunch, during which Brandon was relegated to the background while the women talked clothes and food, a friendship obviously forged.

This had been a fortuitous turn of events, he thought, watching Angie's animated expressions as Robin described a particularly difficult client. Had they left Robin's studio alone, he might have tried to talk Angie into an afternoon that would have been irretrievable. It was good that he'd been forced to take time to think.

Angie was gorgeous. He liked her and he wanted her, but that was all it was. He couldn't give more than that, and she'd made it clear she wouldn't settle for that. So all he had to do was bide his time for two weeks and she'd be gone, back to the wilds of Gray Goose Lake.

And he would have his comfortable pattern back—treadmill, shower, work, dinner with a beautiful, independent woman, sex, sleep and so on.

Yes. That was best.

After lunch, Robin went back to her studio and Brandon and Angie went to buy shoes. They found short, winter white suede booties to go with the cat suit; medium-heeled, brown leather pumps for the suit; and high, patent leather heels for the cocktail dress. Her feet would, naturally, be bare for the nightgown.

Angie was not surprised when Brandon dropped her at home and told her he had to go to the office for a few hours. He helped her carry the parcels in and disappeared more quickly than she could say goodbye.

She'd seen it coming. He'd been distancing himself from her during lunch and had assumed a completely businesslike manner by the time they went shoe shopping.

He didn't want to become any more deeply involved with her, but it seemed to be happening despite what he wanted. The attraction was there, and she was beginning to suspect that it was the real thing, born of the startling way they'd met and the truths about each other they'd been forced to share early on. And they had Mike in common.

It should have been the foundation for something wonderful, but she feared it might not happen at all. And she certainly wasn't going to be the one to push it.

All her life she'd had a sense of being an error in judgment—though it hadn't been until Mike's arrival that she'd understood why. She'd always felt secure in her mother's love, but she'd known that her presence on the dig had been a major inconvenience. When she'd gotten older and had been shipped off to boarding school, she'd wondered why anyone would have a child when the career and life-style she'd chosen made it so difficult.

So Angie had tried to be as little trouble as possible.

And she certainly had no intention of inconveniencing Brandon with something he didn't want to deal with. It was a startlingly painful realization.

Dunston, at least, was happy to see her. He was small and slight, with thinning blond hair and the air of a dandy. But he had a wicked sense of humor and an eagerness to talk. She needed that this afternoon.

"WHAT ARE you doing here?" Mike walked into Brandon's office and sat in the guest chair facing him.

Brandon looked away from the demographics on the computer screen and replied, "I'm vice president in charge of marketing. I'm supposed to be here. You, on the other hand, were supposed to go home in the middle of the afternoon."

"Well, I stayed until six," Mike retorted with a concerned frown, "because I thought you were entertaining Angie. What's wrong?"

Life on the street as a kid had helped Brandon master the "Who, me?" look. "Nothing's wrong. We had her hair done this morning, got some great clothes for the shoot, bought shoes, and I took her home."

"Why didn't you stay with her? She's a stranger here." The question was more of an accusation.

Brandon leaned back in his chair. "Mike," he said

placatingly, "she's a big girl. She probably appreciates a little time to rest."

Mike studied him closely. Brandon tried to close his mind. Mike had always been able to read it, and the skill had annoyed Brandon since he was thirteen.

Mike leaned an elbow on Brandon's desk. "Are you having...you know...sibling problems?"

That was almost funny. "Sibling problems?"

"You know. That's mine. You're in my way. I saw it first. That kind of thing. I still resent my brother Harry taking the sports section when we meet for breakfast."

"No," Brandon said firmly. "We do not resent each other. We had a very amiable morning."

Mike looked pleased. "Good. I wish she would decide to stay, but then her mother would hate me, and I'm hoping we'll be able to be friends for the sake of my relationship with Angie."

Brandon looked back at the computer screen, afraid Mike would see in his eyes that the last thing he needed was for Angie to decide to take up residence near her father.

"Go home," Brandon said, hitting the key to scroll down the screen. "The doctor said you shouldn't be here this late."

"Aren't you coming?"

"Work to do."

"Do it later. I want us all to have dinner together."

"Mike..."

"I'm staying until *you* go home."

Brandon knew he meant it. Mike had manipulated him this way before. He gave a long-suffering sigh, shut down the computer, stood and went to the small closet for his jacket. "You know, you're turning into an old coot," he said, his genuine affection for Mike sounding through the criticism. "When you don't get your own way, you use guilt and cunning to turn things around. That isn't very admirable."

Mike put an arm around him as they left his office. "I'm sort of an invalid. I can be forgiven."

"Hah! When it comes to following the doctor's orders, you're fine. But when you need an edge, you play the invalid. Well, from this moment on, it won't work anymore."

Mike smiled. "Can you not put that into effect until after you drive me home?"

AT 2:54 a.m., Brandon yanked the bunched-up pillow from under his neck, tossed it on the floor and lay flat in the darkness. He remembered from having watched some late-night medical drama that cardiac arrest patients were treated by removing their pillows. He wondered if it worked for victims of *sanity* arrest. In *this* case, it was just another heart problem.

He lay deliberately still and knew after ten seconds that it wasn't going to work, but he stuck it out for five minutes anyway.

When the grandfather clock in the hall below struck 3:00 a.m., he sat up, swung his legs off the bed and headed downstairs for a drink.

ANGIE PACED the living room in T-shirt and knee socks as the clock chimed, marking the inexorable approach of her appearance before the camera. She'd turned on a small reading lamp on an end table to light her path.

What had ever made her think she could model? she wondered. What had ever made her think she could step out from behind a kitchen chopping block and in front of a camera and become a selling tool for a product in need of rescue?

Though many of her classmates in boarding school had had modeling classes, she'd always considered them useless. She'd resisted tryouts for school plays because though becoming involved in a drama had a certain appeal, the thought of remembering lines and the complications of stage movement had seemed daunting.

Public speaking class had been required, but she'd passed without distinguishing herself in any way.

Now her father was depending on her. Brandon was depending on her. They'd been rendered insane, she was sure, by the shock of Mike's discovery that she was his daughter. Otherwise they'd have never chosen her.

It was crazy. She couldn't do it.

But she had to. Professional photographers and studio time were expensive. A lot of people had gone to a lot of trouble. Emilio had styled her hair. Robin had prepared the wardrobe. Brandon had purchased several hundred dollars' worth of shoes.

All because of her *hair,* not because of *her.*

A buzz cut was the only way out.

No. She put both hands over her head and groaned. She had to try. It meant her mother's surgery. She had to remember that.

BRANDON NOTICED a frail light in the living room and detoured from his route to the kitchen, afraid Mike might have gotten up, not feeling well.

He rounded the corner into the room and heard a groan.

But it was Angie, not Mike. She was holding her head and grimacing in pain.

He cleared the few steps between them and caught her arms. "What is it?" he demanded at the same moment that she, startled, jumped and screamed.

He took a step back in surprise, then reclaimed it to put a hand over her mouth as she opened it to scream again. Her wide eyes over his hand closed for a moment with the relief of recognition. She pulled his muting hand from her mouth.

"What—" she began, but he shushed her and listened.

He expected to hear Mike or Dunston come running, but apparently neither had heard the scream. He relaxed and turned to Angie, a bristling annoyance ripe in him.

"What?" he asked, his voice lowered. "I heard you groan, and when I walked in to see what was wrong with you, you screeched at me."

"Well, what do you expect when you sneak up on somebody at three o'clock in the morning?" she whispered harshly. "You should be asleep!"

She wore a cotton nightshirt bearing the logo "Tuxedo Junction" in tall, black lettering, with a white bow tie at the neck of the T. A long expanse of smooth thigh was visible beneath it. Slender calves were sheathed in long, white socks.

Brandon dragged his eyes away from her legs. "Why aren't you?" he asked. Then he noticed how her freckles stood out and her eyes seemed enormous in the pale oval of her face. He said more quietly, coaxingly, "Tell me what's wrong."

She took several paces away from him and spread both arms out, then dropped them to her sides in exasperation. "I'm afraid, okay? You happy now? I have no training for modeling. I'm going to get up there tomorrow, make a complete idiot of myself and cost my father's company all the money you've already spent and whatever it's going to cost for the photographer and the studio. Not to mention that your haircare product line is going to fail."

Angie watched him raise both eyebrows in an expression of amusement. "My," he said. "You're a little harbinger of cheer. Pollyanna would not be pleased with you."

She was watching his eyes because she didn't want to concentrate on the rest of him. He was wearing fleece shorts and nothing else, his long, strong legs bare, his formidable shoulders and torso naked but for an eye-catching, sensual T-pattern of dark hair that crossed his pecs and trailed a line down the center of his chest to disappear into his shorts.

She had to give her head a shake to turn off her imagination, which, no doubt, wanted to pursue what rested at the end of the line.

When she looked up at him again, he still stood casually, hands resting lightly on his hips, but the amusement was gone from his eyes. He'd watched her eyes wander over him and probably read her speculation. His gaze was steady, daring her to deny what had come awake between them at that moment in the quiet shadows of the room.

"I...I can't...model," she said on a raspy whisper, a little tremor beginning in the pit of her stomach and continuing to spiral like the seed of a tornado.

His eyes recognized the ploy to distract him. For one awful moment she thought he wouldn't allow it. Then he folded his arms, but stood his ground.

"Sure, you can," he insisted quietly. "Any woman at peace with herself can model."

She laughed ironically, a little nervously. "Yeah, well, there you have it right there. I can't do this."

"You can. You just have to look the camera in the eye and show it who you are."

She raised both arms again in a gesture of helplessness. "Who I am is a woman who's away from home, out of her element, spending time with a father she didn't know she had, performing duties for which she isn't prepared, under the eyes of a man who—"

She stopped short. She hadn't meant to go that far; the words and the feelings had just kept coming. She spun on her heels and marched into the kitchen. She flipped on the light, picked up the kettle and crossed to the sink with it.

But before she could turn the faucet on, Brandon put a hand over hers and stopped her. He took the kettle from her and put it on the counter, then turned her toward him.

"A man who what?" he asked.

She studied him a moment, searching his dark eyes for a clue to what he felt. When that wasn't clear, she examined herself for some idea of how *she* felt. That was a tangle of confusion, too.

"I don't know," she finally admitted, tired and exasperated. "I haven't a clue. I guess I was trying to say a man who seems to care one moment, but doesn't the next."

He smoothed a hand over the crown of her hair in a gesture at once erotic and tender. It soothed her. Until he spoke.

"I care," he said, "that you're my...benefactor's daughter."

She slapped his hand away, temper sparking instantly. "Bull poop!" she said in a shouted whisper, and tried to stalk past him.

He caught her arm and pulled her back. "Please," he said dryly. "My virgin sensibilities. You're saying you don't believe me?"

"I'm saying—" she drew herself up, the added inch still forcing her to angle up her glare "—that the fearless street kid has grown into a Wilshire Boulevard chicken! My father would probably be thrilled if he thought we had something for each other."

"Yes. He probably would."

She folded her arms, her air superior. "Then that undermines your excuse, doesn't it?"

"No, it doesn't." He dropped his hand from her and turned to walk away.

She caught his arm and pulled him back. Or tried to. He stopped with an impatient huff, but he didn't turn. So she walked around to face him. "Why doesn't it?"

"Because feeling something," he said slowly, as

though she were simple, "and acting on it are very different. I'm not marrying anybody."

She blinked at him. "I don't remember asking you to."

He ran a hand over his face and dragged in a breath. "If I made love to you," he said patiently, "Mike would expect me to be serious about you. And I'm sure he would imagine that ultimately..."

She shifted her weight and groaned again. This time the sound seemed to express anger rather than distress. "Again...I don't recall asking you to make love to me."

His eyes held hers. "You ask me with your eyes every time you look at me."

She opened her mouth to deny that, horrified that she'd been so transparent, but she knew it was useless. She'd always been a poor liar. "All right. I've admitted I find you sexually attractive. But that isn't all it is."

A pleat appeared between his eyebrows. She wasn't sure if it indicated pain or thought. Or was it a thought that hurt?

"I know," he said finally. "That's why I can't act on what *I* feel."

"Because it isn't more than that?"

He smiled grimly. "No. Because it is. And I'm not conditioned to dealing with love and trust."

She felt acute and bitter disappointment. Then she remembered their discussion on the hill the day he and Mike had burst into her life.

"Wait a minute, wait a minute." She frowned at

him. "Aren't you the one who told me that you couldn't remain alone when you knew someone cared about you?"

He remembered that. He hadn't wanted her to turn away from Mike, and he hadn't wanted her to hurt anymore.

He smiled reluctantly. "I don't always practice what I preach."

"So." She drew a deep breath and eyed him with a kind of reproachful tolerance. "I'm expected to be heroic and place myself in front of advertising professionals and a see-all, tell-all camera despite all my fears, but you're allowed to hide behind old childhood demons and ignore *your* fears? Doesn't seem fair to me."

She saw laughter and affection in his eyes, when she'd half expected impatience or annoyance. "Really. Well, what do you think would even up the score?"

"I think—" she looped her arms around his neck and regarded him seriously "—that I should be allowed to force you as close to your fears as you're insisting I go."

There was a moment's silence. Then he asked, "And how close would that be?"

"Another kiss," she said intrepidly, letting herself play with the wiry hair at the back of his neck. She was close enough to see the flare of reaction in his gaze.

He rolled his eyes, pretending disinterest. "All right. If you must."

She let one fingertip drift to his ear and circle the rim, then she leaned into him, letting her softness invade his unmoving muscle. "And while we're kissing," she whispered, "I want you to pay special attention to how strong sexual attraction is heightened further by real feeling."

"But I don't—"

"Shut up," she said softly, standing on tiptoe, her lips reaching for his, "and listen to me."

Brandon hated to do this to her, but he resolved not to react to her efforts to convert him. He would have liked to be the caring lover she wanted, but he didn't have it in him. And if she couldn't take him simply as a lover without strings, then he had to make it clear that there was nowhere to go from here.

So he planted his feet to cradle her body comfortably against his, and he put a hand lightly to her back to help her balance herself on tiptoe in order to reach his mouth. But that was all she was getting from him.

She had to learn sooner or later that her little scheme was hopeless.

He groaned with fatalistic acceptance a moment later when the plan went bad on him. Her lips were warm, her mouth sweet and generous, as she invaded his with a darting, taunting tongue. She planted kisses all over his face; then, with a little sigh that mingled longing and discovery, she plundered his mouth again and this time he had to clench his hands to prevent himself from taking a fistful of her hair and assuming control.

Her hands roved his back; one foot climbed his calf; and when she overbalanced slightly, he took the backs of her thighs in his hands and lifted her until he cradled her bottom in his hands. He had the bunched-up cotton of her shirt in one hand, but round, cool flesh in the other.

After that, he felt as though he were rolling downhill to some inevitable, threatening conclusion.

The kiss heated up, ignited, burned through him like a fire.

She drew back to gasp for air, her legs wrapped around his waist. Her eyes were wide and startled, and he thought for a moment that she wanted to stop, that she was afraid she'd started something she'd lost control of.

But the ghost of a smile teased at her lips. It was filled with tenderness and...happiness. It wasn't a superior, triumphant, ''gotcha'' sort of smile, but a sincere one, filled with honest surprise.

He stared at it a moment, stunned by the knowledge that he'd made her happy. He'd been successful in a hundred ways since Mike had walked into his life, but he didn't know that he'd ever made anyone happy before. The knowledge made oatmeal of his spine.

She drew his head to her breasts and planted kisses in his hair. He ran his lips over the cotton covered protrusions of her nipples and heard her little moan of pleasure.

''Brandon,'' she whispered. She tipped his face up and kissed his eyelids and his cheeks.

He couldn't think.

Then she raised her arms and pulled the nightshirt off. Her small, ivory breasts were revealed to him, nipples pearled and straining toward him.

He took one into his mouth, steadying Angie as she arched against him with a sigh. He moved his mouth to the other, tugging gently until Angie writhed in his arms.

He strode across the living room with her, and into the library. Propping a knee on the brocade sofa, he placed a hand between her shoulder blades and tipped her backward until she lay among a cluster of colorful pillows.

Her eyes as they looked up at him were bright, her skin pale and ethereal in the dark room. He wanted her desperately, but there were cautions to consider here. He couldn't remember them; they existed somewhere on the fringes of his mind, beyond the sensory impact of her naked nearness. He closed his eyes for a moment, trying to think.

Angie remembered that she'd been trying to make a point with this kiss, but she'd forgotten what it was. She knew only that he was warm and responsive, and that when he touched her bare flesh, she felt as though her entire life had been healed. All the empty little corners were filled, and all the dark places illuminated.

He was her answer; she'd known it almost from the beginning.

But she wasn't his answer—or, at least he didn't think so. So now was the time to stop this.

But she wanted to make love with him more than she'd ever wanted anything. Her heart was beating for him at this moment—keeping her alive for no other reason but that she be with him. And though she understood that she'd started this, and that he'd promised nothing, she felt confident that ultimately it would change everything between them. Their connection was so strong, so elemental, that once he really experienced the power of her love for him, he would no longer be able to deny his love for her.

She looped her arms around his neck and tried to draw him down to her.

He resisted, closing his strong, warm hands on her wrists and holding them there. "Angie..." he began on a whisper.

But she sat up to open her mouth over his attempt at reason and kiss it away. She pulled him down to the sofa with her.

He turned as they went down so that she lay atop him in the narrow space. And from that moment on, second thoughts were discarded in the glow of their common first thought—to love each other.

Angie felt herself come alive under his fingertips, but she also felt as though she might dissolve from the tender but proprietary quality of it. It was pleasure and the most delicious pain.

His fingers skimmed her from her forehead to the tops of her socks. He sat up at that point, her bottom perched on his thighs, and ran his hands over the light cable knit that ran from her knees to her toes.

"You want to keep these on?" he asked with a grin in the darkness.

She grinned back. "I'll take them off if you don't mind cold feet against you."

He wanted every inch of her against him. "You won't be uncomfortable?"

"No."

He peeled the socks down, one after the other, then pulled her back down to him again. He explored every curved surface of her body, every warm hollow and every secret place. He kissed her, stroked her, caressed her, and all the while her hair veiled their faces.

Then Angie braced up on her hands and paralyzed him with a line of kisses that began at his lips and trailed down the middle of his body. In the wake of her soft, warm lips were the skimming tips of her hair, like blossoms in the wake of a breeze.

He hoped she would stop at his navel, but she moved on, pulling his shorts down and tossing them aside. His determination to be tender and to make this first encounter last for hours died in its prime.

Her lips touched his manhood and the world and all its mechanisms, himself included, began to speed out of control.

"Oh, Angie," he groaned, half praising, half scolding, as he pulled her up to place her over him.

He saw her innocent grin in the darkness. "Yes?"

He answered the sassy tone of her question by gently dipping a finger inside her, causing her the same instant madness she'd caused him.

She caught him in her hands in response, and they battled it out until she was gasping for him and he needed her with a desperation that was a live-or-die issue.

He lifted her and entered her in one swift, upward thrust that made him as much a part of her as her own heart. In fact, she thought gravely as she felt him fill her—and felt every little corner of her being come to life—he *was* her heart.

But the moment was too physical for the spiritual aspect of it to retain her attention. Pleasure was building inside her, circling, teasing, eluding, then assaulting her again.

Brandon took a firm hold on her hips, arched upward, and pleasure erupted inside her like so many fireworks. Light and color danced around her as her body pursed and opened over his again and again.

Brandon watched the backward tilt of her head, the graceful arch of her throat as climax claimed her, felt the silken sweep of her hair against his thighs, and he suddenly knew the most profound emotional satisfaction. Then her body tightened around his and he lost awareness of everything but his own exquisite pleasure as he exploded inside her.

He felt, too, as though the world exploded. For the moments of his mindless delirium, it was a formless, fragmented mass that made no sense to him.

Then, as he began to reclaim control of himself and his surroundings, it seemed to settle around him again, though not quite as it had been before. Had the darkness held this velvet quality before? Had the air always smelled like flowers? Had he ever been this comfortable with his own body before? And who *was* this fairy-tale woman, that she could bring about such swift and sudden changes.

Angie sank against Brandon as every particle of energy seemed to flow out of her. His arms closed around her and she melted into him, wondering at the strange and convoluted machinations of time and fate that had brought them to this point and place.

She would never say it aloud because she didn't want to gloat, and she didn't want Brandon to know that it was on her mind even now, on the fringes of the wonderful afterglow—but what they had just experienced was so much more than sex.

She could only hope that when he surfaced from his own aftershocks, he would see it, too.

Chapter Nine

"I want you to think sex in the boardroom," Jack Hammond said as he leaned his hands on his knees to study the shot through his camera.

The photographer was tall and lean, with thick, blond hair tied back in a ponytail. He wore one small hoop earring in his left ear, and a perpetual frown.

He stepped away from the camera as Brandon approached him.

"Sex?" Angie asked from her perch on a corner of a desk. "In a boardroom?"

"Sex sells everything." Neil Delaney, the male model hired to be her ad campaign love interest, smiled up at her from the depths of the high-backed leather chair behind the desk.

He was also tall and lanky, and seemed to look perfectly at ease wherever and however he was posed. He had platinum hair, which Angie guessed had been enhanced in the interest of his work, but there was nothing pampered looking about him.

His gray eyes were direct, but could look lazy if that was what the camera wanted. His nose was straight, his mouth thin lipped and mobile, his teeth perfectly symmetrical. He had a cleft in his chin and a smile that could melt metal.

Angie had known him all of forty-five minutes, but thought that for all his physical perfection and relative fame, he seemed nice, intelligent and helpful. She'd learned from the photographer's assistant that Neil had worked in the advertising campaigns for a well-known cereal, a new model of luxury car, a continuing commercial for coffee and one for computer software.

"Well. That amazes me," Angie said, tipping her head from side to side in a vain attempt to relax her neck. "Did I mention that I've never done this before?"

"Four or five times," Neil replied, looking wonderfully indolent but successful in a taupe-colored Armani suit. "Doesn't mean a thing. You've got the look."

"The look?"

"Of woman, friend, lover, devil. It's all in your eyes, and the camera will see it."

"Really." She wasn't so sure. "I think that's terror."

He smiled. "Yes. That's there, too. But you have the look of a woman involved with a man, and that translates to sex for the camera. You'll be fine. Who is he, by the way?"

"Who?"

"The man you're involved with."

She carefully kept all reaction from her face and smiled emptily. "I'm not. I'm visiting from northern California."

He nodded. "Yes. Mike's long-lost daughter. He told me."

When she looked surprised, he explained with a shrug, "I've worked for him before. You'd be gratified to know how thrilled he is."

This time her smile was genuine. "Yes. Well, I'm thrilled, too. He's quite a remarkable man."

"That he is." Neil studied her speculatively. "It's Brandon, isn't it?"

She concentrated on checking her cuff links. "What do you mean?"

"It's Brandon you're involved with."

Angie frowned at him, thinking that she might have some acting talent after all. "Why on earth would you think that?" she demanded good-naturedly.

He leaned his head against the back of the chair and glanced to the sidelines, where Brandon was in deep conversation with Jack and his assistant, a small African-American woman in coveralls.

"Because your glances continually deflect each other's," Neil replied. "And because I've worked with him, too, and he doesn't seem to be quite himself. He seems a little...I don't know. Stunned, maybe."

Stunned. Angie considered that an interesting analysis.

After she and Brandon had made love the night before, he'd carried her up to her room, turned to leave; then, almost as though he were powerless to help himself, he'd made love to her again.

It was dawn when he left her; then he'd greeted her at breakfast as though nothing had happened. But she'd expected that, because Mike had been there.

But when Mike had excused himself to shower, Brandon had turned to her, the passion from last night alive in his eyes. When he'd finally spoken, though, he'd talked about what she could expect today in the studio. And then, when he'd hesitated and she thought he might say something about what they'd shared, he'd excused himself to get dressed.

And so she'd spent every moment since trying to avoid his gaze, afraid everyone would notice that when she looked at him she saw the world in his tall, muscled frame.

It wasn't that she blamed him for anything. She was as responsible for their lovemaking as he—probably more so. She hadn't intended for the kiss to go that far, but they seemed to be volatile together now that they'd admitted to having strong feelings.

She had no regrets, except the superficial one that he hadn't capitulated immediately, hadn't been overcome by adoration for her and an overwhelming thirst for her skillfull lovemaking.

She remained convinced that ultimately, he would see the difference love made in their relationship and he would respond accordingly. In the meantime, all she could do was continue to drive home the lesson.

But not in front of a studio filled with people he worked with.

"He could very well be stunned by the mistake of having chosen me to model for Rapunzel," Angie said, trying to dismiss Neil's observations. "That first shot didn't go well at all."

"You were nervous." Neil patted her hand. "Just

look at me and think of Brandon...or whoever the man is in your eyes."

"Keep your hands off the models, Delaney," Brandon teased as he approached. He wore khaki, cotton twill pants and a tab-collared shirt the same shade. "I've warned you about that before. I'll tell Chantal on you."

Neil closed his eyes, apparently intent on relaxing while there was time. "She went to London last week with Denzel Washington to do *Othello* and I didn't yell at her. She's got nothing to complain about. I think this is personal. You're jealous."

"Shut up and go to sleep."

"I could do that if you'd quit talking to me."

Brandon turned away from Neil, his expression sobering as he faced Angie. His dark eyes went over her feature by feature. "How are you doing?"

He looks relaxed, damn him, she thought. But she made herself reply amiably, "Terrified, thank you. How are you?"

"I told you," he said quietly, taking her hands, "that there's no reason to be frightened. Jack knows you've never done this before, but even he agrees that you're perfect for it." His eyes went over her again in that diagnostic way, then they settled on her eyes and she saw something intimate there, something he probably hadn't intended to share.

He'd taken charge of his life at a very early age, and he'd proceeded through life with a confidence born of that courage. And now he thought he had to remain tough to hold on to what he'd gained; Emilio had been dead-on with his analysis.

But when he looked at her, he didn't appear tough at all. He looked... Neil had said it. Stunned. She wondered if he was remembering last night.

She was. She could see him in his fleece shorts, everything above and below them taut with muscle and resistance. Until she'd looped her arms around his neck.

"Brandon!" Jack called. "Come look at this, see what you think."

Brandon dragged his eyes away from her to nod that he'd be right there. Then he sighed and that vulnerable look was gone.

"You're going to be fine," he said with an encouraging smile. "And if you're brilliant, we'll take you out to dinner and dancing."

Neil sat up. "Me, too?" he asked.

Brandon grinned at him. "Sorry. You're going to be busy tonight."

Neil asked suspiciously, "Doing what?"

"Your answering service just called." He handed Neil a slip of paper. "Chantal's home."

Neil put the note to his heart and smiled unabashedly. "Ah. A walk through Cupid's grove."

"A walk...where?" Angie asked.

Brandon shook his head and backed away. "Don't ask him. He might give you details. All right, you two, no pressure, but be great."

"Okay, let's do this!" Jack shouted.

"Cupid's Grove," Neil said quietly as he resumed what was supposed to be a pompous pose in his chair while he was purportedly distracted by her shapely knees and her Rapunzel hair, "is the...you know... wild thing."

"Oh!" Of course. The wild thing. The wonderful, mind-bending, soul-baring, life-altering wild thing. She knew all about that.

Something sexual entered his smile that wasn't acting. Angie knew he was thinking of Chantal.

He'd told her to pretend he was the man in her life and that the camera would see it. Could that possibly work? she wondered.

She glanced up into the group of a dozen people positioned behind the camera in an irregular curve and spotted Mike and Brandon. Mike blew her an encouraging kiss. Brandon, however, was watching her but not seeing her. His gaze was unfocused, and he was wearing the same smile Neil wore. He *was* thinking of her.

Armed with that knowledge, she approached her role of office Delilah with new confidence.

BRANDON FELT a jab in his ribs and came out of his adolescent reminiscences to the awareness of Mike's whisper.

"Looks like she's getting the hang of it."

Berating himself for not paying attention to business, Brandon focused on Angie and Neil...and was a little startled by what he saw.

Angie had crossed her knees so that her skirt revealed a fairly generous amount of thigh, but her attention was on the notepad balanced on it. She showed the primness Jack had asked for. Her hair, touched up that morning by a young woman Emilio had sent over to stand by, gleamed under the lights and lay about her face and shoulders like an exotic scarf.

"Good!" Jack called. "Now let's see a little awareness of each other."

Brandon watched as Jack placed his forearm on the arm of his chair and leaned on it in her direction. Angie tipped her head only slightly, but all the action was in her cautious glance in his direction.

Brandon felt his heart thump against his ribs. He'd been on the receiving end of that same look. Jealousy reared inside him, dark and fanged, and he forced it down, knowing it was ridiculous.

"Good," Jack said again, sounding a little surprised this time. "Now I want more than awareness. I want out-and-out attraction."

Neil left the chair and sat beside her on the edge of the desk. He took the pad and pen away from her and tossed it behind them. They looked into each other's eyes.

"That's great," Jack said, "but I'm not getting enough of her hair, Neil."

Angie said something to Neil, at which he shook his head. She seemed to be insisting, as he continued to refuse.

"What is it?" Brandon called from behind the camera.

Angie turned to him, her porcelain face illuminated by the lights. "Can I turn my face away from the camera if it lets you see more of my hair?"

Brandon and Mike turned to Jack. He shrugged. "Sure," he said. "We can try anything."

Angie rested her head on Neil's chest, careful to

drape her hair over the shoulder of his suit. "How's that?" she asked.

Jack peered into the back of the camera. He straightened with a raised eyebrow and invited Brandon to check out the shot.

Brandon had done this before, but he always had difficulty translating the upside-down image visible to him to how it would look right side up. But this time he had no trouble at all. The frame was filled with yards of glossy hair, and the only other details visible were Angie's slender fingers on Neil's tie, and Neil's strong chin. It was perfect.

Brandon stepped aside to let Mike see.

Mike straightened, looking pleased. "Take the picture," he said to Jack, "before they lose the pose."

Jack settled behind the camera and immortalized the shot. And the day went on.

Angie, now comfortable with Neil, played off his professional ease with a budding gift of her own. She sparkled when Jack wanted smiles, sizzled when he asked for sex and managed to look regretful when he placed them on opposite sides of the edge of the office door, depicting an attraction that could never be more.

That shot came at the end of the day and jangled Brandon's nerves. And he knew why.

Angie did it so well—her hair hanging in glossy perfection as she leaned her forehead sadly against the door—because she felt it herself. He'd seen it in her eyes several times throughout the day when she'd looked at him.

Neil, with his heroic profile and his look of pensive

grief as he covered her hand on the door with his own, was simply a stand-in for him in her mind.

Brandon felt a lot of things he didn't like—jealousy, anger, resentment, regret. He didn't know why he should. Last night had simply gone beyond what either had intended, but that was attraction among consenting adults. He hadn't spoken of love, but she hadn't tried to stop him. In fact, she'd done a lot more to encourage him.

Tactile memories flooded his brain, raised the gooseflesh on his arms, made him labor for his next breath. He could feel her hands moving over him, making all his resolutions about an emotionally solitary future groan like beams in an earthquake.

"Okay, that's a wrap for today," Jack said, taking a few steps back from the camera and stretching toward the ceiling. "That was good, you two. Really, really good."

Neil came out of character instantly, hugged Angie and kissed her cheek, then ran from the studio, presumably on his way home to Chantal.

But Angie stood alone in the middle of the set, near the door that went nowhere, and seemed lost in the character she and Neil had created. Activity went on all around her as Jack's assistant unplugged cables, a woman from Robin's shop checked the wardrobe rack for the following day's costume and the young woman from Emilio's collected her things.

Brandon felt Angie's tension from a distance. He was grateful when Mike went to enfold her in his embrace and congratulate her on a good day's work.

She smiled up at him, apparently flattered and relieved by his praise.

Brandon was relieved himself. He couldn't stand to
see her in distress, but he knew he couldn't change
the way things were.

At dinner, he did his best to be charming and amusing. He wanted that lost look driven from her eyes.

She wore a vivid blue dress with short sleeves and
a flared skirt. She'd tied her hair back in a long clip
that created a cascade of curly ends. Tendrils dangled
from her temples with a certain wanton charm.

She still wore the makeup from the shoot, and she
looked as though she'd just stepped out of a designer's
salon. It was quite a change from the fresh-faced
young woman who'd claimed his attention on the Gray
Goose Lake Post Office steps, but it looked right
somehow—and seemed to reflect an inside change, as
well.

Learning she had a father had changed her. And he
felt sure that learning she could turn a man inside out
had also given her a certain confidence she hadn't had
before.

After dinner, Mike took her onto the dance floor.
Brandon couldn't deny the pleasure he felt in seeing
them together. Mike glowed with the new gift of holding his daughter in his arms, and she sparkled like a
jewel. Their mingled laughter drifted back to Brandon,
and for the first time in years he felt left out. It was
one thing to be alone by choice, but quite another to
be alone because you didn't fit in. He noticed, also,
that he didn't like the feeling.

He topped off his glass of Merlot from the carafe

on the table, wondering what in the hell was wrong with him. It wasn't like him to pout. He guessed he was experiencing guilt because he'd made love to Mike's daughter in Mike's home. He wasn't quite as sure as Angie was that Mike would be thrilled at the prospect of an alliance between his daughter and his foster son.

After all, Angie was his blood, the result of a love liaison during an unforgettable summer.

Brandon knew his presence in Mike's life was the result of Mike's loneliness and social conscience. Brandon's father had died in jail. He doubted that was a legacy Mike wanted for Angie.

"Dance?"

Brandon was jolted out of his thoughts by the presence of Angie's small hand held in front of his eyes.

"Dad was stolen from me by a buxom matron wearing emeralds and diamonds," she explained, waving a hand casually in Mike's direction. Then she challenged Brandon with her eyes, their green looking aquamarine above the vivid blue dress. "Would you like to dance, or shall I sit this one out?"

He pushed himself from the table, stood and took her hand. He knew he shouldn't do this. The moment he had her in his arms he'd want more from her than he knew he should have, but he was skating on the edge tonight—torn between compliance with the demands of good conscience and the memory of the scrappy kid so determined to survive his parents' legacy of crime and poverty that he was fearless.

Angie felt the infinitesimal tremor in him when he turned on the corner of the dance floor and she walked into his arms. It echoed inside her as she looped her arms around his neck and leaned into him, pressing her temple against his chin.

She remembered in sensory detail their bodies touching the night before, her breasts crushed into his sturdy rib cage, the sensitive skin of her stomach deliciously abraded by the wiry line of hair down the middle of his body, the flesh of her bottom molded in his hands.

She sighed at the memory.

Brandon tried to take her left arm from around him, to assume the more traditional dance posture, but she knew he was simply trying to force distance between them, and she refused to allow it.

She'd been good in front of the camera today. And she saw no reason she couldn't put that seductive skill to good use in her real life.

Brandon finally took hold of her upper arms and forced her a step back. He glanced around them with a thunderous brow to make sure no one noticed their altercation. But the dancers were all busy with their own dreamy contemplations.

"You're forgetting your father," he whispered warningly, pulling her back into his arms and catching her left hand before she could put it around his neck. "He doesn't know that…"

"Yes, he does," she said, her tone matter-of-fact. "I told him."

"What?" He stopped and dropped both hands from her.

She shushed him and wrapped both arms around his

neck. "You're making a scene, Prinz," she said. "Dance. The violinist is staring at us."

The other dancers were too busy to notice them, but the people still at the tables were looking their way.

Brandon wrapped his arms around her waist because he had no choice, and he tried to move his feet in some semblance of rhythm to the R and B tune. "I don't *believe* you would do that!" he said under his breath.

She kissed his cheek and leaned into him again. "Will you relax? He was pleased."

Her floral scent surrounded him, penetrated his brain and tried to turn him from his annoyance. He resisted. "He wasn't pleased. He just didn't want to risk losing your affection by pointing out that I'm a poor risk romantically."

"That's ridiculous."

"That's the truth."

"That you're a poor risk romantically? I know that, but if I'm willing to take the chance I don't see why you shouldn't be. And it is true that Dad was pleased. I can't believe you think he wouldn't be. He loves you as though you were his own son."

Brandon looked down at her, resisting a desperate need to shake her. "We'll talk about it later," he said firmly.

"What's wrong with now?" she asked, nuzzling his chin.

"Witnesses," he replied shortly.

Chapter Ten

"My father," Brandon said emphatically, "died in jail!"

He paced Mike's study while Mike poured brandy into three balloon glasses. Mike hesitated over the third glass. "I know that. I shot hoops with you for three hours straight after we got the news, because you were determined not to let it mean anything. Is Angie joining us?"

Brandon had ripped off his jacket and now pulled impatiently at his tie. "I sent her to her room," he said absently.

Mike grinned. "I'm new at this father thing, but isn't that supposed to be my job?"

Brandon huffed impatiently and leaned a hip against the back of the sofa. "You know what I mean. I told her I wanted to talk to you and asked her to stay out of the way. She went to her room on her own."

"Well." Mike ignored the third glass and carried the second to Brandon. "If you put it that graciously, it's small wonder. I thought after years of trying, I'd finally gotten through to you on the importance of tact. You're in marketing, for God's sake."

Brandon took a deep gulp of brandy and walked across the room to look out at the lights of Beverly Hills down the hill. "You might want to discuss the tact thing with her. She's the one who blurted out to you that we slept together."

There was a moment's heavy silence. Brandon turned, an awful suspicion dawning on him.

Mike had sobered slightly, though he didn't look angry. He sat in his chair and kicked the hassock toward Brandon, gesturing that he should sit on it. "Actually, she didn't. All she told me was that she was falling in love with you, and she thought you were falling in love with her."

Brandon swore, ran a hand down his face and moved to comply. "Look, I'm sorry. I know *I* should have told you, but I hadn't intended for it to happen, and now that it has…"

Mike shook his head. "You should never have to apologize for loving someone." His eyes gentled on Brandon with a compassion he remembered as the first sign of light in his life when he'd seen it all those years ago. "Did you think that I wouldn't want her to be with you?"

Brandon leaned his elbows on his bent knees, the glass dangling between them from his fingertips. "My father died while doing twenty years in San Quentin, Mike."

"You keep saying that," Mike observed, taking a sip of brandy. "I don't see how it applies."

"Speculating ahead," Brandon tried to explain, "what do I tell our children when they ask about their grandparents?"

Mike toasted him with his brandy. "That I'm alive and well. At least, I hope I will be."

Brandon sighed with forbearance. "That's good. Then, when Angie tells them she comes from the same father, they're going to really be confused about the family tree. You have been like a father to me, Mike, but it isn't your blood in my veins—it's Marty Prinz's, three-time loser."

This time Mike sighed, and there was an edge of temper in it. "Blood and DNA make the package, but what's inside you makes up the product. You've been in business long enough to know that."

"Yes," Brandon replied, getting to his feet. "And I've been in marketing long enough to know that packaging goes a long way toward selling the product."

"The first time. But the quality of the product makes the second sale. And don't argue with me." Mike downed his brandy, then gave him that look that could still make him compliant. "You know damned well what you're made of. If you want to lean on that blood crap because you're afraid of getting any more involved with Angie, then admit it. But don't use it as some noble excuse, because neither of us is buying it."

Brandon paced away from Mike toward the window, stared broodingly through it for a moment, then paced back again. "I have strong feelings for Angie, but I don't know that I have it in me to love her."

"You've loved me."

"You didn't ask for anything. You took what I could give. A woman should be loved generously."

Mike gave him a pitying shake of his head. "Brandon, the fact that you know that means you can do it. But you're the one who has to understand it. Do you want to walk away from her, never knowing what you could have had? The way I did with her mother?''

Brandon swallowed the last gulp of brandy and went to put the glass on the bar with a firm thunk. Then he turned to Mike with a sigh. ''No. I'm afraid the painful truth is that now that I've made love to her, I don't want to walk away from her, ever. But I don't want to hurt her, either.''

Mike's mouth twisted wryly. ''That's what I thought about Gretta all those years ago—that separation would be better than trying to merge our divergent life-styles. Now I see with the clarity of hindsight that I should have fought harder for a solution. I found Ruthie and that was wonderful—I wouldn't change that. But I missed my daughter's entire childhood. I wasn't there for her mother.''

''Because she wouldn't let you be.''

''I should have fought to be. In fact, I've decided that it still isn't too late to go into battle.''

Brandon stopped in his pacing to turn and frown at him. ''What do you mean?''

Mike pushed himself out of his chair. ''I mean I'm going back to Gray Goose Lake and bring Gretta back here for a while. I'm going to try to talk Angie into staying, and I think she'll be more receptive if I can get Gretta to stay. So I have to be on good terms with her.''

Brandon bit back a smile. ''That could be dangerous. Is anyone on good terms with Gretta?''

Mike smiled reminiscently. ''I used to be once. And

I'd like to be again.'' Then he focused on Brandon, put an arm around his shoulders and walked him to the door of the study. "Trust me, Son. You can't pass on love. You have too much heart. And you have my blessing. I can't think of a better way to face my future than with the two of you united in yours.'' He pulled Brandon to him and hugged him fiercely. "You're just the man I'd want for her if I could select him myself.'' Then he let him go and pushed him toward the stairs. "Now, get out of here. I'm leaving the rest of the shoot in your hands. I'll probably be gone for a few days, so take good care of Angie.''

"Right.''

Angie, however, seemed to be determined to make those instructions as difficult as possible to follow. When Brandon knocked on her bedroom door, she told him to go away.

"I'd like to talk to you," he said reasonably.

"Yeah?" came her reply. "Well, I don't want to talk to you.''

He didn't know what had brought about this sudden change of mood from the temptress on the dance floor, but he knew how to get around her. "It's about your father," he said.

She pulled the door open several inches and asked anxiously, "What about my father?" Her face was pale, her hair loose. She'd changed out of her dinner dress and into her nightshirt. "Is he all right?"

"He's fine.''

"Then what about him?"

"Let me in and I'll tell you," he bargained.

She considered him for a moment, as though she'd

never seen him before, as though she hadn't melted in his arms the night before or tried to seduce him on the dance floor an hour earlier.

She finally pulled the door open all the way and let him in.

Guests had always liked this room above the garden because it was wide and deep and had room for a small, flowered sofa and a desk and chair near the window. Also, when the French windows were open, as they were now, the scent of roses wafted up and brought the fragrance of the garden in.

But he wasn't thinking of furnishings or roses now. He was thinking of Angie, and how a man explained to a woman that he wasn't sure he could love her, but that he couldn't imagine his life without her in it.

Of course, the temper he read on her face when she closed the door behind him and came to the middle of the room to confront him suggested that discussing their relationship was a moot point anyway.

So he did the cowardly thing and worked around it. "Mike's going away for a few days," he said, wandering toward the bed, where her dress and some lacy underthings lay.

She followed him. "Why? Is he not feeling well?"

"No, he's fine." He picked up the lacy bra and studied its fragile construction with interest. "He's going back to the lake to get your mother."

She snatched the bra away from him, but he saw that last statement reclaim her attention. She looked first concerned, then pleased, then concerned again. "You're teasing me!" she accused.

He picked up the panties, no more substantial than a handkerchief. "Not yet, I'm not."

She yanked those away from him, too. "Has he called her?"

"No, I don't think so. I believe he intends to surprise her."

"Well..." She did that frowning-smiling thing again. "What makes him think she'll come?"

He leaned a shoulder against the tall post at the foot of her bed. "I suppose he intends to be persuasive."

She put a hand to her eyes and groaned. "I hope he knows what he's doing. She can be pretty testy when she wants to be."

"No kidding." His response was quiet and dry. "I couldn't have guessed that by the way you've inherited the quality. Apparently, he had a way with her once. He seems to think he can recapture that."

Suddenly her attention refocused from her father to him. She put her hands on her hips and took an aggressive stance. She was wearing knee socks, so she must not have been expecting him.

"Is that all?" she asked.

"That's all about your father," he replied.

With a brisk yank, she took the dress off the bed and went to the wardrobe with it. "My father was all I wanted to talk about. You may go now."

He held his ground. "I'm not ready to go."

She turned away from the closet, her eyes sparking as she glanced up from fiddling with an apparently uncooperative hanger. "I hope you didn't force your way in here figuring you were going to share my bed."

He smiled, thinking this wasn't the way he'd imagined love at all. He'd thought it would be warm and comforting, rather than prickly and energizing. It wasn't so much solace as...rejuvenation. He could almost feel the electrical impulses from his brain, the mechanisms that moved his muscles, the drumming of his heartbeat.

"No," he said. "I didn't expect to share your bed."

She seemed to take exception to his smile. She shoved the dress in the closet, part of it still dangling from the hanger, then slammed the closet door.

"That's good," she said, advancing on him, cheeks pink, hair flying, "because I've decided I don't want anything to do with you after all."

"Really." He felt curiously calm. This was just temper. He was getting used to it. "Come to your senses, have you?"

"Yes!" she said.

The index finger of her right hand was pointing toward the ceiling; he was sure it could have impaled plaster had she been tall enough.

"I have no interest in a man who is embarrassed by a little demonstration of affection in public," she added.

"Angie," he said placatingly, knowing it would only further annoy her, "you were within seconds of undressing me on the dance floor."

She rolled her eyes and turned away from him in exasperation. "You wish! How male of you! I had myself under complete control!"

"The way you do now?" he asked quietly.

She bristled. She obviously wanted to hit him, and

he found himself almost wishing she'd try. He felt rather physical himself.

But she kept her distance. This time she pointed her index finger at herself. "I'm sorry. I'm just not the cold fish you are when it comes to passion! I don't stop to analyze what might hurt me and what might not—what part of this is temporary and what part is permanent, and what that will ultimately mean to my *peace of mind.*" The last few words were spoken several decibels higher than the others, then she drew a breath and lowered her voice again to add, "I just do it and decide that if it all goes to hell on me, I'll survive. I'm a big girl."

Angie wasn't sure what she'd said in that loud and lengthy diatribe that made a look of challenge flash in his eyes, but something had. He straightened away from the bedpost, suddenly a very different man from the one who'd entered the room. The comfortable indolence was gone and his hands were now out of his pockets.

He came toward her, and it was all she could do not to back away.

"Cold fish?" He repeated her words quietly but with disputing emphasis. "I pause to give this relationship a little thought because your father literally saved my life and because I'd die before I hurt him— or you—and for that you call me a cold fish?"

He towered over her in her stocking feet, and she could feel the warmth from his body, feel the heat from the sparks in his eyes. She fought the impulse to lean backward and out of his way.

"Why don't you just admit you're afraid of me,"

she said with as much disdain as she could muster under the circumstances.

With a sudden movement he caught a fistful of her hair, and she wondered for an instant if she might have gotten the who-was-afraid-of-whom part a little backward. Then he lowered his mouth on hers and she didn't have the time or energy to think about anything.

He took everything she had. Every breath, every particle of strength, every ounce of her personal power.

She wanted to think that she gave it, entrusted it, but after last night her body seemed to now belong to him rather than her. It leaned into him without asking her for instructions—her arms automatically rising to circle his neck, her mouth opening for him and giving him everything he wanted.

Everywhere his hands touched, her flesh tingled in response. And the deep, velvet heart of her that wanted so much to enfold him again grew heavy and liquid with longing.

When she expected to faint from lack of air, he drew her head back and asked again, his voice a little thin, "Cold fish?"

She dragged in a breath. "I take it back," she whispered. "But why were you angry that I told my father we were falling in love?"

He smiled thinly. "Because I thought you'd told him we'd slept together. And I'd wanted to break it to him."

"I didn't tell him that," she denied.

She'd kept that bit of information to herself not out

of deception, but out of reverence for the newness of
it.

He nodded ruefully. "I know. I blundered into that
myself, thinking you had."

She leaned back in his arms to look into his eyes,
sure that now that her father knew, he was pleased
rather than horrified. "I don't understand, Brandon.
Why did you think he wouldn't be pleased? You know
how much he loves you."

He usually managed to put this out of his mind, but
he'd had to say it several times tonight, and it appeared
he'd have to say it one more time.

"My mother was a druggie, Angie," he said, as
though trying to impress upon her the importance of
that in their situation. "She left when I was very small,
and I have no idea what happened to her. And my
father died in prison for participating in an armed rob-
bery in which a bank guard died."

She met his gaze evenly. "That's awful, but what
does it have to do with you? With us?"

"Well…thinking ahead a little…how would we explain that to our children? If you decided this is really
love. If we got married. If we *had* children."

She was careful not to let him see how thrilled she
was that he was thinking in those terms—marriage,
children. She pretended confusion. "I don't see why
you're worried about it. You keep telling me you don't
think you can love me."

He gave her a look that told her he knew she was
working him. She feigned innocence.

"I know what I've been telling you," he said, running a hand gently up her spine, "but I also know

that…I don't know what's happening. Something's changing.''

"What?"

"I said I don't know."

"Well, do you think I'd risk my future on a man who doesn't know what he feels?"

She saw his eyes darken. "Does that mean you want to end it here?" he asked.

This was the dangerous moment. She had to give him his open door. "No," she said, looking into his eyes and letting him see how serious she was. "I want to hold on to you until I can convert you. Now, knowing that, what do *you* want?"

He considered her for a moment, and she felt her heart constrict with the awful premonition that he was going to turn and walk away.

Instead, he swept her up into his arms. "I want," he said, "what I came in here for."

Deliriously happy, she forced herself to remain calm. "You told me you didn't come in here intending to share my bed."

"I didn't," he replied, walking to the door with her and turning sideways so he could go through it. "I wanted to take you back to mine."

THEY MADE LOVE so long that the makeup artist tsked as she put concealer under Angie's eyes to cover the dark circles.

"It makes no sense," she said, "that you have circles under your eyes, yet your eyes themselves are bright and clear. It took me an hour and a half to make

Neil look like a living human being. What do you people *do* when you leave here?"

"We partied with friends," Neil said softly to her as Jack's assistant arranged a fern on the marble fireplace mantel behind them. Angie was wearing the turtle-necked, winter white cat suit, and Jack had borrowed a friend's Gothic sitting room in Bel Air for the afternoon. "Then we partied alone. I didn't close my eyes until four."

Neil looked closely at her from their hip-to-hip position on the bear rug in front of the hearth. "Hmm. You're wearing concealer. You mustn't have gotten much sleep, either."

Angie ignored that observation and plucked at the sleeve of his thick, black sweater. "Aren't you roasting in that? I feel like I'm about to expire from the heat."

Neil raised his eyebrows with an erudite air. "Professionalism, my dear. A good model never sweats until the shoot is over."

Jack shouted instructions at them. "Okay, kids. Think of this as a stolen weekend in a remote hideaway far from Neil's wife and Angie's demanding neurosurgery practice."

Everyone on the set laughed.

"Want a lobotomy?" Angie asked Neil as he put a hand under her hair and drew her face toward his, letting her hair fall over his arm and to its best advantage for the camera.

"Maybe later," he said. "What I really want now is a corned beef sandwich on Russian rye."

The shot was perfect, but Brandon couldn't look at

it. The sight of Angie in Neil Delaney's arms filled him with a killing rage he recognized as completely ridiculous, but dangerous all the same.

He stayed all afternoon as Angie and Neil moved from one cozy clinch to another—apparently, judging by their laughter, having a great time together. They seemed to have established an easy camaraderie that worked wonders for the shoot, but was fracturing Brandon's good humor.

Angie noticed that he was testy when they got home that evening. Dunston had made a wonderful cappellini-with-shrimp dish, with a side salad filled with mysterious greens and avocado and topped with a lime vinaigrette that was so light and delicious she teasingly threatened to bathe in it.

Brandon, his plate empty, pushed away from the table in a decidedly quarrelsome mood. "While you're playing queen of the Nile," he said abruptly, "I'll be in Mike's study. Thanks, Dunny. Great dinner."

"Don't you want dessert?" Dunston asked, turning from the counter with a goblet of bread pudding in each hand. Angie had seen Dunston toss it with *crème anglaise*, and couldn't imagine a sane person turning it down.

Brandon snatched the goblet in Dunston's right hand. "I'll take it with me, thanks."

"Leave mine on the table, please," Angie asked the butler. "I'll be right back."

She caught Brandon halfway across the living room. "Is something wrong?" she inquired, puzzled by his attitude. He'd been this way since the middle of the afternoon when she'd asked him about the fireplace during a break. His reply had been abrupt and bad tempered. "I thought things went well this afternoon."

He gave her a quick condemning glance that changed to one of disinterest. "Did you? I suppose Neil has turned you into an expert overnight?"

She took instant offense. "What does that mean?"

"Which word was too big?" he asked, walking away from her.

She raced to keep up with him and stop him at the stairs. She yanked him around by his shirtsleeve.

"The only thing too big around here," she said, "seems to be your ego. Are you implying that I'm pretending to know more than I could on such short exposure to studio work? Or are you suggesting that Neil and I are...more than acting?"

"The choice is yours," he replied calmly, pulling away from her. "Take them both."

"That's stupid and childish!"

"Funny. That's what I thought."

He pulled his arm away and loped upstairs. She went back to the kitchen, snatched her pudding and spoon off the table and went out to the garden. She sat on a stone bench and glowered at the lights of downtown Beverly Hills, just coming on.

Dunston brought her a napkin and a cup of coffee. "Don't chew the glass," he advised her, regarding the goblet. "Those are Venetian."

"What's the matter with him?" she grumbled at the butler.

He shook his head. "Uncertainty, I think," he said. "He doesn't like it. I haven't seen this behavior in him since he was a teenager. Except for those few days when Mike was in the hospital, and we weren't certain how serious his condition was or how much damage had been done. He just doesn't like to not know what he's doing. And love does that to a man.''

She wasn't surprised Dunston knew. He seemed to read everyone's mind.

She sighed. ''He insists he doesn't know what he's feeling.''

''Of course he does.'' Dunston flicked an insect off the leaf of a rose. ''He just doesn't know what to call it. Don't crowd him. He'll be fine.''

Oh, good, Angie thought, devouring the pudding as though it were some prey she'd hunted down and caught with her bare hands. *But how will I be?* The tension between them seemed to have accelerated rather than eased with that curious truce forged the night before. What did that mean? she wondered. That this would work between them, or that it wouldn't? She couldn't decide.

As dusk ripened into darkness, she returned the goblet and spoon to the kitchen. Dunston was cleaning vegetables, the cordless phone cradled on his shoulder. ''Yes,'' he was saying. ''Yes, she's right here. Hold a moment, please.''

He handed the phone to her and shooed her out of the kitchen as the dishwasher turned onto a noisy cycle. She settled on the living-room sofa.

''Hello?''

''Angie, what is your father doing here?'' her mother demanded.

''Mom!'' Angie was happy to hear her voice,

though dismayed at the anxious sound of it. "Hi! How are you?"

"I'm fine, thank you," came the quick reply, "but don't change the subject. Why did you send your father here?"

"I didn't!"

There was a loud silence, then Gretta repeated, "Then why is he here?"

Angie struggled for patience. "I'm sure if you ask him, he'll explain."

"Oh, he's already tried. I just don't believe him. He says he's come for me. Well, why does he want me? He's already got you. It doesn't make sense."

Angie decided she liked the stress in her mother's voice after all. It meant she was uncertain, confused. There was satisfaction in knowing misery had company.

"Of course it does," she said patiently, "if you consider that I'm not the only woman he wants in his life."

The line was silent again. Then her mother said in a small voice, "He says he wants me to see his home, to visit Southern California."

"Do you want to come?"

"I hate cities!" she grumbled, then after a moment's silence asked shortly, "Do *you* want me to come?"

That would be an out for her, Angie guessed. She could tell Mike she was coming because Angie wanted her to. "Sure," she replied. "I'd love to see you."

There was a sigh. Relief, Angie knew. "All right, then," her mother said. "I'll come."

Angie returned the phone to its kitchen cradle and warned the butler with a grin, "Seems there'll be four for dinner tomorrow night, Dunston. My father is bringing my mother home."

He lopped the knobby heads off three carrots with an efficient stroke of a lethal-looking knife. "That sounds like a natural turn of events."

She leaned an elbow on the pristine, white counter-top and watched him decapitate three more carrots. A veritable harvest of garden vegetables was colorfully strewn around his chopping board.

"My parents hadn't seen each other since I was conceived," she said moodily, wondering what would come of her mother's visit, "until he came to the lake last week."

The notion that they might reunite after all this time had all the fluffy foundation of a fairy tale. But there was a fragile hope in her that it would happen.

But that was crazy.

Dunston went to the pantry and returned with a box of vegetable storage bags. "So he told me. But things have a way of turning out the way they're supposed to be, despite all our efforts to plot our own destiny."

Angie dropped the headless carrots into the bag he held open. "You don't think we're in charge of our own destinies?"

"Sort of," he replied. "I think certain good things are ordained for all of us, but we decide whether or not we achieve what's planned."

She considered that and decided that as an expla-nation of fate, it was as good as any she'd heard.

She zipped the bag closed for him while he sliced

the tops off red and yellow peppers. "You must have majored in the culinary arts and minored in philosophy," she teased.

He smiled, reaching into a pepper to pull out its seedy heart. "Living makes philosophers of us all—if we're paying attention."

She glanced in the direction of the stairs. "*Cranky* philosophers of some of us."

"The wounded are more cautious," he said, slicing the pepper into neat rings. "It has to make you grumpy to look at all the world's wonderful things and not be able to just grab them because previous experience has taught you that it can be dangerous."

Angie bagged the pepper rings for him and had to admit that that was true. Feeling guilty because she'd snapped at Brandon when she might have defused their argument with a little effort, she kissed Dunston's cheek, then headed off to the study.

Brandon wasn't there. She walked through the living and dining rooms, checked the family room with its big-screen television and overstuffed furniture, the gym off the garage, and did a quick stroll through the garden.

She ran upstairs and looked into his room. It was dark, but there was an oblong of light from the bathroom at the far end. She heard the splash of water. "Brandon?" she called, taking one step into the bedroom.

For a moment there was no answer, then he called back, "Yeah?" still sounding a little remote.

"Are you okay?"

Another hesitation. "Why wouldn't I be?"

"Well...no reason. I just couldn't find you, and you...um...don't seem like the type to loll in the tub."

"I'm not lolling. I'm bathing."

"In lime vinaigrette?" she teased.

He asked in a voice softened with amusement, "You want to nibble on me and find out?"

That was tempting, but she took only one more step into the dark bedroom. "Aren't you in there because you need privacy?"

"I'm in here," he replied, his tone self-deprecating, "because I needed to cool off. Would you come in here so I don't have to keep shouting at you?"

Angie went as far as the doorway and peered inside. The room still bore an old ball-and-claw bathtub. It had been painted dark blue to match the blue and white towels and the vertical blinds. Across the width of the tub was a wire rack that held soap, the empty bread pudding goblet and spoon and a Larry McMurtry novel.

Brandon reclined in the clear water, his wet feet crossed atop the rim of the tub on the faucet end, his head resting against the head of the tub. The humidity in the room had curled the hair at his temples, and he held a lit cigar in his teeth. He looked very much like a bandit relaxing after some satisfying thievery.

She leaned a shoulder in the doorway and studied him in surprise. "I didn't know you smoked!"

He took the cigar from his mouth. "I quit three years ago," he said, then put it back in again and spoke around it. "But I still have a stash of good cigars for moments of stress and times of personal stupidity."

"So, which are you now? Stressed or stupid?"

"Both." Water splashed around him as he drew his feet in and sat up, his tan pectorals now visible above the rim of the tub. His expression was wryly apologetic as he took the cigar out of his mouth again. "I'm sorry I snapped at you. I had to watch Neil holding you and nuzzling you all day. It made me want to kill him. Since our backward society considers that socially unacceptable behavior, I snarled at you, instead."

She walked into the bathroom and knelt on the white carpet at the head of the tub. She kissed his warm, moist shoulder. "Well, jealous and stupid aren't exactly the same thing."

He leaned sideways to kiss her mouth, his eyes grave. "It occurred to me while I was sitting here that if I don't have a claim on you," he said, "I don't have the right to be jealous."

She reached to the tray across the tub and took the bar of fragrant herbal soap. "That's true," she said, moving the soap across his back between his shoulder blades. "Although 'claim' is a word I'd use carefully if I were you."

"You know what I mean." He bent his knees and leaned over them to allow her room to work. "*Commitment* is used and overused. I know it remains the issue. I'm just tired of the word."

She worked the bar of soap down his spine, then dropped it onto the tray and worked the soap in with her hand.

"All right. 'Claim' it is. Then I've *claimed* you, so you really don't have to worry about being jealous, because I'm quite monogamous." She scooped up water with her hands and poured it over his back. Then she took a towel from the rack and patted it dry.

"So you don't need that." She took the cigar from between his thumb and forefinger and carried it to the sink, where she poured cold water on it.

"Hey!" he complained.

Sure it was saturated, she dropped it in the wastebasket. Dusting her hands off, she returned to the tub. "Do you want to cut short what promises to be a long and wonderful life?"

He leaned back to look up at her, his eyes depthless. "Are you going to be in it?"

He wanted desperately to hear a "yes," but he knew he'd made that impossible. She shrugged the shoulder of a simple, white, cotton T-shirt. "I guess at this point that's undetermined. But, with or without me, do you want to die before your time?"

He guessed "his time" would be the moment she left him.

"No," he replied.

"Then don't whine about the cigar," she said. "And we've settled the jealousy issue, anyway."

He grinned up into her eyes. "But what about my stress?"

She grinned back, holding a towel open for him. "I was planning to take care of that when you get out of the tub."

He pushed the tray out of the way, then reached for the towel and used it to pull her down to him. "Why *out* of the tub?"

"Brandon!" she protested, laughing. "I'm dressed!"

Another deft yank and she landed on top of him on her back with a squeal of laughter. He had her unbuttoned, unzipped, unhooked and unclothed in a matter of seconds.

"This tub is too small," she protested, giggling now as he helped her turn over.

"That's not a problem," he said, pulling her up along his body so that he could claim her lips and feel her body melt into his.

It happened in an instant. "Why not?" she asked, the whispered question lanquid even as she found space for her knees on either side of him.

"We're stackable," he explained on a husky note and smoothly entered her.

Chapter Eleven

"You ready?" Neil asked Angie.

They stood in a dance pose in front of the six-member dance band of the Downtown Club in West Hollywood, who were rehearsing for that night's show. Jack stood off behind the glaring lights, the rest of their now-familiar entourage ranged around him.

Angie wore the flirty pink dress with the cutout spot just under her breasts. "Ready for what?" she asked anxiously. She'd known him just long enough to be ready for anything.

"I'm going to dip you," he said.

She smiled hopefully. "In chocolate?"

"In the dance," he corrected with a playful glare at her for her absurdity.

"All right, guys," Jack called, "I'm ready, so let's have action. We want her hair to fly, Neil!"

The base counted off a rhythmic "one, two, three, four" and the band erupted into a brassy, energetic tune Angie didn't recognize.

Held firmly in Neil's arms, she was led across the front of the bandstand in a series of high-movement steps in compliance with Jack's instructions. Her hair did indeed fly as Neil twirled her, flung her out to the tips of his fingers, then brought her in once more.

They danced their way back again, then Neil asked again, "Ready?"

"Can we reconsider the chocolate?" she asked in reply.

His answer was a firm grip on her that tipped her backward, while keeping himself out of the frame.

"Hold it!" Jack shouted. "That's great!"

Brandon watched from the side of the set and knew that shot would be a winner. Angie's hair streamed like strands of dark copper, catching and refracting the studio lights.

The saucy pink dress clung lovingly to her breasts, her bare neck stretched long and sacrificial. He knew every inch of that neck and those beautifully molded shoulders, he thought with a new kind of peace that hadn't killed his jealousy, but made it easier to live with.

"My God!" Gretta whispered, standing beside him. "What if he drops her on her head?"

"He won't," Mike assured her. "He's a pro. This kind of shoot's a lot of work for the male model because he's essentially a prop, but he's done everything he can to make Angie look good. Not that she needs much help. She has a natural talent for modeling."

Gretta frowned worriedly at Angie as Jack continued to shoot. "She seems to be having fun."

"I think she is," he said. Mike caught Brandon's eye over Gretta's head. "Wouldn't you say she's enjoying L.A.?"

"Ah...yes, I would." Brandon gave the answer he

knew Mike was hoping for. Mike and Gretta had arrived from the airport only an hour ago, but it was already obvious that Mike was on an all-out campaign to prepare Gretta for the possibility that Angie might stay—though, to Brandon's knowledge, Angie hadn't reached that conclusion herself.

Gretta moved a few feet forward and to the side for a better view.

"You're pushing this a little hard, Mike," Brandon cautioned quietly. "Did Angie say she wants to stay?"

"She said she was in love with you," Mike reminded him. "Isn't that the same thing?"

Brandon shook his head over how much his benefactor had to learn about today's woman.

"No. In fact, she keeps analyzing Dunston's desserts and talking about all the new things she's going to try in the tearoom when she gets home."

"Well, I'm going to fix that," Mike said with an air of certainty that caused Brandon a nudge of concern.

"How?" he asked.

"You'll see as soon as we're done with the shoot."

"All *right!*" Jack shouted over the music. "I've got it! You two were brilliant." He left the camera to hug Angie, shake Neil's hand, then speak to the club owner, who'd arranged for their intrusion into rehearsal.

Neil hurried off and Angie shaded her eyes against the lights. Mike shouted to her and she ran at her mother with a cry of excitement. "Mom, hi! How was your flight? Isn't this fun?"

"Hi. Fine. Yes," Gretta replied in rapid order. "You even look like you know what you're doing."

Angie dismissed that with a wrinkle of her nose. "Neil does all the work. All I do is toss my hair around."

"Which looks gorgeous, by the way," Gretta said, putting her gnarled hand to Emilio's angled style. "It makes you look...like a big-city girl." Gretta frowned as she said the words.

"Nah," she said, wrinkling her nose again. "Still me inside. How're things at the shop?"

"Great. Becky and her sister seem to be doing fine. Those customers who've complained about missing the variations in menu were appeased when we told them what you were doing. But they're expecting you back."

"Well, of course. Dad?" Angie turned from her mother to Mike. "Can we take Mom to Percival's, where you took me that first day of shooting?"

Brandon watched Mike quickly school his expression from the worried look his features had taken on at Angie's talk of going home to one of enthused indulgence when she looked at him.

"Of course. And the day after tomorrow we'll take her shopping. Tomorrow's the last day we can have Jack, so we've got to stay with the schedule."

"Please," Gretta said. "Don't change anything on my account. I just wanted to...look around. I can wander on my own tomorrow."

Mike shook his head. "Absolutely not. I'll take you where you want to go."

"Mike." Gretta made a disapproving face. "You're

dealing with a woman who's been to the wilds of the African bush. I think I'll be fine in Beverly Hills.''

He granted her that with a nod. "I have no doubt you would be. But I didn't bring you back here so that you could take off on me. I want to show you around. We'll leave the kids to do the last day of shooting by themselves."

Slightly mollified, Gretta shrugged a shoulder and nodded. "All right. That'll be nice."

"Whoa," Angie said quietly to Brandon as they walked arm in arm behind her parents toward the car. She'd doffed the pink dress and wore white jeans and a black T-shirt. "Dad's coming on strong."

"I know." Brandon frowned, beginning to worry about him. "I think he has an agenda we don't know anything about."

Angie laughed throatily. "Or maybe he just remembers what it's like to deal with Mom. Unless you drop a piano on her, she doesn't stop to listen to you."

"No, I DON'T dance well." Gretta tried to refuse Mike's suggestion that they join the couples on the dance floor. "My knee joints are stiff and I get rickety."

Mike pulled her chair back. "They're playing 'Sentimental Journey.' I don't think that's going to call for any acrobatics on your part."

"Shall we call Neil?" Angie joked.

Ignoring Gretta's protests, Mike pulled her gently to her feet. "I think I can handle this myself. Remember, Gretta, when the Gray Goose Dance Palladium stood at the end of the pier? And you could hear the music all the..." The reminiscence faded away as Mike led Gretta slowly onto the dance floor.

Angie watched them go, her chin on her hand. "Aren't they cute?" she asked Brandon. "I'll bet they were quite a couple when they were young."

He turned to study Mike and Gretta—the tall, slender gray-haired man and the small woman who moved with care but smiled widely once she turned into his arms. He felt that nudge of alarm again. Something was going to blow here; he had a good nose for trouble.

"They're a handsome couple now," he said.

She folded her arms on the table and smiled dreamily. "Wouldn't it be something if this all came out right in the end like some...some fairy tale?"

It worried him that she was thinking in those terms. A fairy tale for selling hair-care products was one thing. But in real life?

Still, he couldn't look into her eyes, alight with the possibility of finally having two parents, and suggest to her that it might not happen.

He caught her hand and pulled her to her feet. "Yes, it would. But we have our own fairy tale going. It's time for the ball at the castle."

She laughed as he led her onto the dance floor. "Wrong fairy tale. I'm Rapunzel, remember. I'm locked in a tower. What did I do to deserve that, anyway?"

"I think you were too beautiful, and the witch was trying to keep you from the eyes of men."

She made a face. "Well, that's a reach," she said.

He looked into her upturned, freckled face and saw

there the world he'd dreamed of as a child. "No, it isn't," he said as he took her into his arms. "Not at all."

Angie leaned her forehead against his chin and moved with him to the music, trying to ignore the subtle but persistent impression that something was not quite right. She hadn't a clue what it was. Her father was being charming, her mother was behaving very civilly for her and Brandon kept looking at her, Angie, with a possessiveness that was thrilling but just a little worrisome. It reminded her of the tenacity of a man who knew he was about to lose something.

Perhaps it was because the week was almost over. They would have to part then; she had a business to run and he was vital to Rampion Pharmaceuticals. If he could admit that he loved her, she would close the tearoom in a minute and come back to stay. But if he couldn't, she didn't want to settle for lover status. She wanted the unity her childhood had denied her.

And then, of course, there was the issue of her mother. She would have to come along if Angie relocated—and her mother hated big cities. Or so she said. She seemed to be having a pretty good time in this one so far.

But that crossroad was still a few days away. For now Angie would be happy in Brandon's arms.

When he didn't come to her room after everyone had gone to bed and the house was quiet, she went to his, and found him standing moodily by the window in the fleece shorts he wore to bed. He was holding the drape back with one hand and sipping something from a barrel glass in the other.

Tomorrow—or rather later today—was the last day of work in the studio. She hoped selfishly that he was struggling with his feelings and deciding he couldn't live without her.

"Are you all right?" she asked, putting a gentle hand to his bare back. She felt warmth and tensile muscle—and a rigidity that communicated itself to her.

He let the drapery go and hooked that arm around her neck to bring her close to him. "Why are you still up?" he asked, ignoring her question.

"Because I've gotten used to falling asleep in your arms," she said, leaning into his shoulder and planting a kiss there.

"It's late, Angie," he said. "You're going to look ragged for the camera."

She nipped his collarbone. "Doesn't matter. I'm modeling a negligee. I'm supposed to look sleepy."

He smiled, put the brandy down and lifted her into his arms. She leaned into him contentedly—until he left his room and carried her back into hers.

She felt a jolt of alarm. Was this...rejection? Not just for the moment, but forever?

Even as she worried over that thought, he placed her in the middle of her bed and bent over her to kiss her deeply. She felt raw emotion in him, and undeniable passion for her.

Then he drew away to pull her covers over her and left the room.

Thoroughly confused, she stared at the ceiling until dawn.

THE SIGHT of Angie in the negligee in Neil's arms was more than Brandon could take without making a scene. The set was a bed with silk sheets, the coverlets folded back invitingly, and a Queen Anne chair with a wedding dress and a tux jacket tossed over it.

Brandon was tempted to leave, but he made himself stay as a kind of punishment for having been the one who'd set this all up in the first place.

"Okay, kids!" Jack shouted from behind the camera positioned at the foot of the bed, everyone strung in the familiar irregular line on either side of him. Neil's and Angie's performances and antics had turned work to fun for all involved—except Brandon. "You've come straight from your wedding reception with one thing on your minds. Let's have it."

Neil and Angie must have talked it over beforehand, because they didn't give Jack the kiss everyone expected. Instead Angie put her arm around Neil's neck, her hair draped over it, and they simply looked into each other's eyes.

The moment, though obviously carefully calculated, had an ingenuousness the camera—and therefore, the buying public—would love. It spoke of excitement, anticipation, promise—all the things marriage claimed to offer.

All the things that had died in Brandon years ago.

Mike had rescued him from hunger and the violence of the street, and replaced that experience with love and security and every advantage he needed for personal success.

What he couldn't replace was the bud of giving that grew and flowered when a child was small, then carried him into adult relationships. When he'd tried to relate to his father as a child, he'd been smacked, ignored and eventually abandoned when his father had been arrested.

He often felt that part of him was like salted ground. Nothing would grow there ever again.

As Brandon watched the shoot, his gut burning with his own deficiencies, Neil swept Angie into his arms, then placed her on the bed so that her hair hung over the foot of it. Then he leaned toward her from the side, dutifully giving her center stage in the shot so that the camera framed her glorious hair, the artful and interesting furrow of her brow and only his adoring profile.

Brandon turned on his heel and left the studio.

ANGIE WAS SURPRISED when her parents picked her up at the studio. Mike said Brandon was taking care of a crisis at the office and would be tied up until late.

Angie accepted the news graciously, but felt her confusion of last night deteriorate into anxious concern. She had a suspicion she and Rapunzel would not share a happily-ever-after ending after all.

Yet there was a wonderful reward to the past week's events that she hadn't imagined in the beginning. Today her parents had, apparently, found something of the old spark that had brought them together years ago—the spark that had been responsible for her life.

Her father and mother smiled at each other across the table as her mother recounted stories of their day's exploration of Los Angeles. She was animated and glowing, and, suddenly, a new threat interposed itself between her parents' happiness and her own.

The shoe was now on the other foot—and it wasn't Cinderella's. What if her *mother* chose to stay and Angie couldn't?

"I thought you didn't like big cities?" Angie reminded her as she speared a bite of lobster.

Her father reached across the table to cut her mother's chicken and she didn't *mind*. She'd always been so sensitive about help when Angie had tried to offer it.

"This one's different," her mother said. She wore a simple, pale blue silk shift Angie had bought her in Gray Goose Lake, and though it probably wasn't high-life wear, her sparkling eyes gave her whole appearance a festive look. "It's so much cleaner than I expected, and so interesting. We toured Hollywood and Universal Studios, and the warm sun on my back made me feel ten years younger. It's too bad the Olduvai isn't in L.A. I feel so good I could probably work again."

A bittersweet acceptance began to settle inside Angie.

She heard Brandon come home after one, and she mentally tracked his progress into the cool, dark bedroom. She imagined him pulling off his jacket and tie, unbuttoning his shirt, doffing the rest of his clothes and walking on long, muscled legs into the bathroom.

She heard the sound of water running in the tub and wondered if he felt the need to cool off again. If he needed his back scrubbed.

Clear images of the other night ran through her mind and caused a languid lust to pool inside her where he had been.

Impatient with herself, she turned onto her stomach, pulled the sheet over her head and forced herself to think about the tea shop and what she would have to do when she got back.

But it didn't work. All she could envision was lying atop his body, filled with his manhood; warm water lapping about them as a pleasure as much spiritual as it had been physical turned her blood to fire.

"YOU LOOK like you've been kneaded," her mother observed as Angie joined her and Mike and Brandon at the breakfast table. "Maybe slapped against the table one too many times." She put a kinked hand to Angie's forehead. "Are you all right?"

Angie drew a breath, taking a moment to collect herself, then raised her head to give everyone—including Brandon—a smile. She would die before she ever let him know she was convinced he was about to hurt her.

"I'm fine," she said with a dramatic wince. "I had insomnia last night. I guess it must have been letdown now that the shoot's over."

Dunston came to the table with a glass of orange juice. "Drink that," he ordered gently. "I want you wide-awake for my breakfast quiche."

Mike gave Brandon a look of surprise. "We never get breakfast quiche. How come we never get breakfast quiche, Dunny?"

Dunston patted her father's shoulder. "Because your diet doesn't allow it, and Brandon, the peasant, has eaten nothing but bacon and eggs and sourdough toast for almost twenty years."

Gretta frowned at Brandon. "That'll kill you, you know."

He smiled and shook his head. "Nah. The stress of business will get me first. Here, Angie," he said, pouring coffee into her cup. "What you need to get started is some down-and-dirty caffeine."

She glanced at him with a casual "Thank you," look and was instantly stalled in her movements by a look in his eyes that offered all the things she'd been sure he'd decided he couldn't give.

For a moment she simply stared at him. Fortunately, Dunston had gone back to the kitchen and her parents were deeply involved in a discussion about the tyrannical nature of nutritional reporting.

Brandon sat at a right angle to her and pushed her now-filled cup closer. "Good morning," he said quietly, his eyes warm and caressing. "Drink up."

She put the juice down and took a sip of coffee, hoping the caffeine would clear her brain, settle a sudden flutter of nerves. Was she imagining that look in his eyes?

She glanced at him again.

No. Lust and affection were curiously combined in a look that traced her face like a fingertip. She felt the night's tension ebb away. Still, she tried to hold on to caution. He hadn't said anything—but, of course, he couldn't with her parents at the table.

"Good morning," she replied, smiling back. "We missed you at dinner."

He nodded, his gaze caressing her again. "That's handled."

The promise in that assurance seemed to suggest

that all was well. But she was afraid to trust that feeling entirely until she heard the words. And that would have to wait until tonight. Mike had planned a day of shopping and sight-seeing.

Unwilling to let Brandon think her life hinged on his ability to love her, she smiled brightly at him. "Good," she said. "You can help me pack the four-feet-tall Mickey Mouse I bought for Becky."

He patted her hand and sat back as Dunston carried a steaming tray to the table. "You can ship that, you know," he said.

And stay behind herself? That was hopeful.

"I thought I'd carry it on the plane," she persisted.

He opened his mouth, whether to dispute that or approve it she wasn't sure, because the table was suddenly abuzz with conversation as Dunston wondered if anyone needed anything else, Mike asked her to pass the pepper and Gretta sniffed the bacon and cheese quiche, went into raptures and proposed to Dunston.

Chapter Twelve

"Look." Angie cornered her father in Saks between
the accessories and the shoes. A clerk at the counter
was delirious with the amount of her sale and was
soliciting help from the other clerks to box and bag it.
"You can*not* keep doing this. If you want to buy
things for Mom, that's fine, but you *have* to stop buying things for me. I've got the clothes from the shoot,
you bought me a hat and a purse and a—"

"Angie." Her father placed his hand heavily on her
shoulder, but she guessed it was simply to get her
attention. The look in his eyes was light and amused.
"I'm the dad. I can do whatever I want. That's something you'll have to understand about having me
around."

She leaned her cheek against his hand but shook her
head at him warningly. "That attitude will last about
as long as it takes for you to try to issue an order to
Mom."

He pulled Angie into his arms and crushed her
close. "I know that, but God! I can't tell you what it
means to me to have her back in my life again. To
have you." He tightened his grip as he added the last.

"And to know that you and Brandon might just... round out the circle. What have I done to be so blessed?"

Angie clung to him, wondering what her life would have been like had he been a presence in it. Would she and her mother have lived at the dig? Would she have had to go to boarding school? Probably not.

There was little point in speculating, she supposed, because those things had made her what she was and nothing could change it now, just as Brandon's childhood had shaped him so that nothing could make love and trust easy for him.

They had lunch in the dining room of the Sunshine Hotel, a Victorian beauty somehow saved from developers and tucked away on a side street in Beverly Hills, close enough to downtown to be noticed, but far enough away to provide the intimacy a comfortable inn and restaurant required.

The elegant dining room was filled with local business people, Angie noticed—a good sign that it was well patronized.

Angie turned down the dessert tray. "I'm not going to fit into anything you've bought me when I get home." The remark about going home was added to persecute Brandon, who hadn't taken an opportunity to pull Angie aside and explain that look in his eyes. "Or will I need energy for what you have planned this afternoon?" she asked her father. "We've bought one of everything in town. What's next? Tiffany's?"

At her question, a short, stout, mustachioed gentleman appeared, whom Mike introduced as Charles Giacomonte, the proprietor of the hotel.

"He has something to show you," Mike said, pushing away from the table and encouraging everyone to join him.

Angie raised a curious eyebrow at Brandon as her father and his friend led the way.

Brandon put an arm around her and ushered her along. "You'll like this," he said. "Gretta?" He offered her his free hand as they climbed three steps at the far end of the restaurant. They passed through a short, carpeted hallway and reached double glass doors.

Charles opened them, then closed them again when everyone was inside, cutting off the sounds of conversation from the restaurant.

Angie found herself in a spacious conservatory at the back of the hotel. The glass enclosure was semicircular in shape, with a terrazzo floor, round wrought-iron, glass-topped tables and spindly legged chairs, and several tall, potted palms near the glass wall that fronted the sidewalk. A dozen ferns hung on pulleys high up in the glass-domed roof so that they could be lowered for watering.

It was a magical place, she thought, imagining the laughter and conversation that would have sounded here in the days when the hotel had been built.

"When my great-grandfather opened the hotel," the proprietor said, "this was an extension of the restaurant and guests loved to breakfast here. Today, we lease it out because my children aren't interested in the hotel, and I have all I can manage with the main dining room."

Angie was lost in images of corseted ladies in ruffles and lace and gentlemen in celluloid collars, sipping coffee and tea while they read the newspaper.

"What do you think?" Mike asked.

Angie shrugged. "It goes without saying. It's a beautiful spot."

"I mean," he said, "what do you think of it as a location for the Tintagel Tearoom?"

"Mike!" Gretta turned on him in surprise, her tone scolding.

He shook his head, dismissing her displeasure. "I know, I know. You don't want me to try to lure her here, because you think I'm just going to let the two of you go back home and live your lives, while I carry on with mine as though we all haven't made a momentous discovery in one another."

"Dad, I..." Angie, dealing with complete surprise, entertained the totally terrifying thought that this *would* be a lovely spot for the tearoom.

"I'll leave you to talk it over," Charles said, withdrawing to the doors. "Mike, give me a call."

Mike waved an assent.

Then he turned back to Angie. "You don't have to decide today," he said, his expression changing from determination to vague sheepishness. "Charlie will wait until tomorrow. After that, a bagel franchise wants to move in, and though that isn't what he wants for this spot, he has to lease it. So you can have tonight to think it over."

"Tonight!" Gretta complained. "That's high-handed even for the man who flew to the lake to drag me back here."

"I'm not letting her go without a fight, Gretta,"

Mike said firmly. "And you, either. I don't expect you to change your whole lives for me, but I *can't* go to you. I have hundreds of employees dependent upon me. I can't just sell out. So, I think in the interest of according me some special favor, since this was all your doing in the first place, Gretta, I think you can come to me."

Gretta huffed impatiently. "You always think the way you want things is the simple way, the right way. But Angie's already turned her life around once to accommodate *me*. Now you want her to pull up stakes again?"

He gave Gretta a superior look. Angie thought it matched the statement he'd made in the shop about being the dad and doing whatever he wanted. "I'm not the one," he noted quietly, "who kept her existence from me, causing us to spend her lifetime apart."

Gretta's mutinous expression matched the warning Angie had given her father after he'd made the statement.

"I did that," she said with dangerously soft vehemence, "for you. I knew if you knew about her, you'd feel obligated to stay with me, and I was going to Africa."

He made a scornful sound. "Listen to yourself, Gretta. You did it for *you*, because you didn't want me to make you stay!"

"You couldn't have *made* me do anything then," Gretta retorted, "and you can't make me do it *now!*" And she turned to march away with her careful gait, then stopped and turned back to Angie. "Would you like to come with me?"

At that moment, Angie couldn't have said what she wanted. The surprise of this wonderful room, the prospect of moving to Beverly Hills—something she hadn't really seriously considered because everything had been too uncertain—and her parents' argument after the days of warm closeness left her head and her heart spinning.

"No," she said finally. "I need a few minutes."

Gretta stalked off.

Mike looked uncertain for a moment, then took off after her, pointing to Brandon. "Talk Angie into it, Brandon. I'll meet you back at the house."

When the glass doors closed behind Mike, quiet settled over the glass-domed room. Angie felt a little like a figure in a snow globe—one that had just been turned upside down.

Brandon remained quietly beside her, his arm still around her shoulders. It was a little difficult for her to take in all that had happened in such a short space of time.

She looked up at him. "Did you know he was going to do this?"

"Yes," he admitted, leading her toward one of the small tables. He pulled a chair out for her and sat her down. He sat opposite her, the table so small, her nose could have touched his.

He still wore that look of intense passion mingled with deep affection. "I'd like you to stay, Angie."

The words gave her a feeling of warm comfort and

relief, at the same time that the quick downward sweep of his eyes brought a warning.

"Why?" she made herself ask.

He raised his gaze to hers again and held it. "Because I don't think I can live without you."

That wasn't quite good enough. "And *why* is that?"

"Because I think about you all the time," he replied without hesitation, his eyes roving her face, hungry and needful. "Because I dream about you, because even when you aren't in my arms I can still feel you there, because...I had to leave the shoot yesterday when Neil put you on the bed."

Angie looked deeply into his eyes and, curiously, despite all the words of love, saw the end of everything. He was holding back the one thing she wanted to hear with every control at his disposal.

She leaned back in her chair. It didn't put much physical distance between them, but she figured the emotional chasm was already there. "But you don't want to think in permanent terms," she said.

He closed his eyes a moment, then opened them and reached for her hand on the table. She drew it back.

"I don't want to make a vow to you," he explained, his voice tight and anguished, "to do something of which I am incapable."

She was now annoyed beyond reason. Love for him prevented her from hating him, but it didn't stop her from wanting to beat him to a pulp. Civility, however, required that she do it verbally.

"Then why do you want me to stay?" she demanded.

He sighed, as though certain what he was about to

say wouldn't make her happy. "Because there's no reason we can't live together."

Brandon watched her eyes and tried to gauge her reaction. They were dark green with temper, but her face was quiet, a pale little freckled mask of neutrality. He could see that she was angry, but behind the anger there was love for him—strong, pulsing, deeply rooted love.

"And how would that be different from being married? I'd be the same. You'd be the same."

He sighed. "Yes. But I wouldn't have promised you anything."

"Do you think it would hurt any less when you walked away," she asked, getting to her feet, "because you hadn't promised you'd stay?"

"How do you know I'd walk away?" he asked.

"Because you won't promise you'll stay!" she screamed back at him. "God! With that turn of mind you've become a captain of industry?"

He caught her arm, the table still between them. He was rapidly losing track of the argument that had made sense last night when he'd thought it through, but now seemed shaky at best. He just knew he couldn't let her go.

"Would you please listen without the histrionics?" he asked sharply, hoping the need to fight would hold her in place.

He'd been right. She squared her shoulders and gave him a withering look. "I suppose to someone reluctant to feel anything, emotion seems like histrionics, but to those of us who don't deal with demographics and consumer profiles but with *real people*..." She bellowed those words, then drew a breath and continued more quietly, "Feelings erupt and we can't help it. But never fear. I won't inflict my histrionics on you any further. What I felt for you just died an untimely but merciful death."

He felt as though he'd taken a knife to his own heart, but he made a final effort to shake her resolve. "Because of a suggestion that we live together?" he asked, continuing to hold her still when she tried to shake him off. "Maybe you need to get out of the tearoom, Miss Corwin, and into the present."

She kicked him in the shin with a ruthlessness that made his eyes water and would have brought a groan to his lips if he wasn't so determined not to flinch— physically or emotionally. And if he didn't know he deserved it.

"No," she said, angling her chin.

A tear spilled from her eyes anyway, and his own pain was suddenly not limited to his shin. He was in agony everywhere.

"I know that works fine for many people, but it wouldn't work for me. I've had a fine life—I won't deny that—and though I've loved everyone in it and don't blame anyone for anything, it was never the life I wanted. I wanted an *entire* family. I wanted a mother *and* a father who were *with* me, not halfway around the world. I wanted to live in a house, not a boarding school, and..." She drew a breath and finished in a voice barely held together, "I want that for my children. I want them to have a father, not just the man who's their mother's lover. Goodbye, Brandon."

He let her walk away because he didn't know how

to hold her, short of physical force. With all his being, he wanted to be the man she wanted, but in the quiet times when he examined what he'd accomplished and who he'd become, he knew that, despite his successes, at the heart of him was still the closed-up, angry kid. And he just couldn't give himself to Angie on her wedding day.

As the glass doors closed behind her, his life literally darkened, and the beautiful, sunlit conservatory became an ice cave.

ANGIE TOOK a cab home, numb now that the pain had overpowered even her ability to feel it.

She went in search of her father, hoping to find a way to explain why she had to leave, and heard his voice as she approached the study. It was raised in what sounded like desperate frustration.

Angie could also hear her mother sobbing. She stopped near the door, unwilling to interrupt their argument, but upset by the anguish she heard coming from each of them.

"You're absolutely right." Her father's voice filtered to her through the door that had been pulled inward, but not closed. "I had no right to spring that on her, but damn it, Gretta, you stomped all over my rights when you kept her birth from me. So I'm taking a few things upon myself, whether I'm entitled to or not.

"When she was born, you made all the decisions. Well, this time I'm making them. You're staying with me, you're having the surgery on your hands, I'm taking you somewhere warm and tropical to recuperate and Angie's going to use the money she made modeling on her tearoom.''

"Mike..."

"I don't want to hear it, Gretta. I won't push her into anything. I want her to stay here more than anything, but I know she's a grown woman with a mind of her own, and I think..."

He hesitated and Angie heard a grumbled sigh.

"I think something's wrong between her and Brandon."

Her mother sniffed. "I noticed that."

"He was a great kid, who became a fine man against incredible odds. But he still has some old issues. I'm not sure why that is, but it's something I don't seem to be able to help with."

"I like him," Gretta said.

"Everybody likes him. Father Saldana thinks he's a saint. And I was happy that he and Angie fell in love. It made it all so perfect."

Angie felt her heart rip right down the middle. She knocked quickly on the study door before she had to think about that another minute. She pushed it open slightly and peered around the door.

Her mother sat wrapped in a robe in her father's chair, and he, in casual navy slacks and a sweater, sat on the hassock.

"Can I come in for a minute?" she asked.

"Sure," her mother replied with a frail smile. "We're just shouting at each other. We haven't gotten to hurling threats yet." She cast Mike a dry glance. "Just a few ultimatums."

Angie nodded. "I know. I heard them as I walked

up the hall. Listen.'' She came up behind her father and put her arms around his neck. He caught her hands and brought them to his lips. ''I have something to tell you.''

''I know.'' Mike forestalled her. ''I'm despotic, with delusions of grandeur. Your mother told me.''

She leaned over him to kiss his cheek. It occurred to her as he held her hands in his strong, paternal grip how much she would miss him. ''I think you're kind and loving and charming, and you're right to make Mom stay with you. You've recaptured that old love. You probably never lost it—it was always there, waiting for you to catch up. But...''

Mike's eyes sharpened, as though he sensed danger.

Her mother stood, so that they formed an anxious little knot in the middle of the room.

''What?'' he asked. She guessed that he knew, because everything about him pleaded with her not to say it.

So she did it quickly, clearly, so there'd be no mistake. ''I have to go, Dad. Mom. And I'm going to do it now before Brandon comes home.''

''What?'' her mother demanded. ''Angelyn Corwin, you are not going back.''

Angie hooked an arm around her mother's neck and kissed her cheek, knowing the bravado for what it was. ''It's okay, Mom. I know you want to stay. I'll be fine at the lake by myself. I lived on my own for four years after college, remember?'' She'd hated it, but no one needed to know that.

Mike came closer to take both of them in his arms. ''You had a fight with Brandon,'' he guessed.

She nodded, her throat too tight for a moment to emit sounds. "Yes," she said finally. "He doesn't want to make promises he thinks he can't keep, and...I know it's very unsophisticated of me, but I *need* promises. I have to know that I can count on him."

"Angie, it's only been a little over a week. Maybe if you gave it more time..."

Angie shook her head and drew a deep breath to steady her fragile composure. "No. We were connected immediately and we both knew it. More time wouldn't make him able to let himself love me, and it wouldn't stop me from loving him."

Mike shook his head, close to tears himself. "The damnable thing is...you *would* be able to count on him. He doesn't understand what the man in him has become. He just remembers the kid."

Angie nodded. "I know that, but he doesn't. And you need him here. So...I can't stay. Please understand."

Mike pulled her close and her mother closed in so that they shared one very belated, but thorough, embrace. They wept together.

BRANDON RAPPED on Mike's office door the following morning. He'd spent the night at his condo in Malibu, staring at the moonlight on the waves and wondering what in the hell to do with himself. He felt like a fatal wound, showered and shaved and somehow moving around on two legs.

Mike took one look at him, tapped the intercom button with a curt "Hold my calls" and pointed to the chair facing his desk. "Sit down before you fall down."

Brandon unbuttoned his suit jacket and complied, happy to be off his feet. His head was pounding; his eyes felt as though he'd combed them along with his hair; and because his heart ached, everything ached.

"You might have called," Mike said, leaning back in his chair, "to let me know you were all right."

Brandon propped one foot on the other knee and closed his eyes, needing a moment's dark peace. "You knew I was all right," he said. "I'm not thirteen anymore."

"Really." Even through closed eyes, Brandon could tell Mike was analyzing him. "I didn't know *you* were aware of that."

Brandon wasn't sure what that meant, only that he wasn't in the mood to spar. He opened his eyes, folded his arms and cleared his throat. "I've decided to move out," he said rapidly, before he could think twice about it or change his mind. "I only moved in so you wouldn't be alone while you were recovering from your heart attack, and...well...you're fine now, and with the ladies there, I feel in the way."

"I'm sorry." Mike looked surprised—a little theatrically so. "I thought we were all getting along so well."

Okay. He knew. Brandon backpedaled. "Angie told you we had a fight."

"Yes."

"Well. I think she'll be more comfortable with you if I'm not around. In fact...you know...I was thinking I'd take a month off, maybe go to Europe and mull over a new product or something while I'm touring. The hair-care line was the only area where we really needed help, and I'm sure this campaign will put it on its feet. So I'll just kick back for a while."

Mike nodded pensively. "Sure. You're welcome to go if you want to. It's very noble of you to want to leave the field clear, but rather unnecessary."

Brandon frowned. "What do you mean?"

"I mean the house isn't that crowded anymore. There's only one lady in it."

"Gretta went home?"

"No," Mike said quietly. "Angie did."

Brandon felt as though Mike Tyson had given him a right to the jaw. Everything inside him rattled. It was one thing to know he and Angie couldn't be to-gether—it was one thing for him to consider putting an ocean between them, but it was something else en-tirely to know she was *gone,* that there were five hun-dred miles of mountains and valleys between them.

"But...she loved the old hotel's conservatory," he said, getting to his feet and walking around Mike's desk to the window. "I could see it in her eyes. She wanted to lease it."

Brandon heard Mike's calm voice behind him. "But she wanted something else even more, and when she understood she couldn't have it, she thought the best thing to do was leave."

Brandon stalked away from the window and went to stand in front of the desk. "That makes absolutely no sense," he said.

Mike shrugged. "A lot of things—and people— don't. But they exist anyway."

Brandon wasn't too rattled to hear the suggestion of an accusation in that calmly spoken bit of philosophy. He put his hands in the pockets of his slacks and demanded combatively, "Is there something you'd like to say to me?"

Mike stood and faced him across the desk, the sudden release of spent patience in his quick movement. "Yes!" he said, pointing a finger at him. "You're being a jerk, and as I recall, a jerk is *not* what I raised! You have been there every time I, or Dunston, or Emilio, or any of your other friends needed you without having promised them anything."

"Mike—"

"And furthermore, has it occurred to you that while you're taking the noble position of not wanting to inflict yourself upon her because you can't promise to open up, or be there, or whatever the hell your problem is, that you're forcing *her* to live without you anyway. Forgive me, but the favor you think you're doing her escapes me!"

Brandon stood still, sorting through Mike's words for the message he couldn't quite grasp.

"And you want to know something else?"

"No."

Mike ignored the negative, opened a manila envelope that lay on his desk and spilled out four eight-by-ten color photos. "Come and look at the face of the man who claims he can't love. Jack sent a couple of contact sheets, but these are his personal favorites."

"Mike—"

"Get over here!"

"All right!"

Brandon walked around the desk. Mike kicked his chair back and moved aside so that Brandon could look at the photographs of the Rapunzel shoot spread out on his desk.

Even in a temper, even carrying the weight of his anguish, even knowing that the future lay black and interminable ahead of him, he had to smile.

The first photograph was the office shot in the power suit. Jack had not chosen the one where Angie had flared her hair over Neil's shoulder, but the one where Neil remained in his chair and she'd simply glanced at him. The moment was alive with electric attraction—and her Emilio-magic hair looked magnificent.

Mike pushed the second one toward him—the white cat suit in front of the fireplace. Neil had threaded both hands into her hair, which fell over his near arm like fire spun into thread. Her profile was delicate and intense. He'd seen her look just like that so many times.

Pain ripped through his middle, but Mike tossed another photo on his desk blotter. "The wedding-night scene," Mike said.

The silk sheets shimmered in the photo, but Angie's hair gleamed even more brightly as she lay on her back on the bed, her hair dangling over the edge, long and liquid and seductive as the shot's theme.

"Beautiful," Brandon admitted, his voice strained, his mind playing back moments of their lovemaking that his memory had immortalized—her hair streaming over him, her breasts small and perfect in his hands, her porcelain skin above him, around him, enfolding him. The need to roar with pain almost overwhelmed him.

"But this is the one," Mike said, pushing it toward him, "that says it all. Jack thought we might even leave you in as a drama bonus we hadn't planned."

It took Brandon a moment to figure out what he was talking about. It was the shot at the Downtown Club with the band in the background. He remembered it clearly, because Angie and Neil had been laughing as they danced, and their laughter had infected the crew. Neil's foot had caught in a light cable, and Brandon had gone back behind the band to reconnect it.

Neil and Angie were twirling along the front of the bandstand, Neil's arms held in perfect ballroom style, Angie's high-heeled foot and stockinged leg poised as gracefully as a ballerina's between Neil's legs. The flirty skirt of the pink dress flared, and Angie's hair swept out and around her, swirling into her face as she laughed.

And then he saw it. A small image in the far right corner of the shadowed edges of the shot. His face.

He remembered the moment. After reconnecting the cable, he'd remained there, afraid of intercepting their twirling rush across the frame. Angie had caught his eye and aimed her laugh at him, and he'd felt it pour through him like so much tangible sunshine.

He was smiling. But it was the look in his eyes that said it all. They were soppily indulgent; shamelessly lovesick; deeply, profoundly, lost in her smile. And if he'd ever wondered precisely what love was, he had his answer there in his own face.

He stared at the image of Angie, remembering what

had prompted that look in him, rocked now by what it all meant.

"She had caught my eye," he said, his voice sounding frail and curiously alien to his own ear. "And she aimed her laughter at me. I felt so...warm. And I smiled back, thinking that if I could give her back a fraction of what she made me feel...I'd be happy."

Mike turned Brandon toward him and leaned forward pugnaciously until they were almost nose to nose. "Well, Son," he said, his voice rough with momentous authority, "what in the hell do you think love is?"

Chapter Thirteen

Becky Flynn stood over Angie while she tore up chunks of egg bread and arranged them in three oblong pans, then sprinkled currants over the top. It was midmorning, and the coffee-break rush was over and the goodies-to-go-with-lunch rush hadn't begun.

"What are you making?" Becky asked.

"Bread...pudding," Angie replied, a catch in her throat breaking the words apart. She remembered the night she'd eaten hers in the garden after quarreling with Brandon, then making up with him in the tub. Pain and loss wrenched her insides. She ignored them. She was going to have to learn to live with them. "It's my father's cook's recipe. You'll love it."

There was silence for a moment, then Becky put an arm around Angie's shoulders. "What happened while you were there, Angie?"

Angie turned away from her to reach for the eggs, sugar, cream, rum and vanilla she'd already whisked in a bowl.

"I modeled for a famous fashion photographer," Angie replied, pouring the mixture over the bread. "And made enough money to put all those lunch things on the menu that I've been wanting to add, and, if they go over well, to expand into the next shop.''

Becky patted her shoulder. "I know. I love your hair. You should go into a business where it doesn't have to be stuffed under a hat all the time.''

Angie patted the chef's hat she wore. "Well, I won't be able to go back to Emilio's to have it restyled, so it'll be its old shaggy self before long.''

"But what I really wanted to know,'' Becky went on with cautious concern, "is...did everything go okay with your dad?''

Angie nodded, turning away from Becky to carry two of the pans to her large oven, where pans half-filled with water already waited. She put the cake pans carefully inside. "Beautifully. He's wonderful.'' The pain and loss swelled inside her as though her memories acted as a kind of yeast. She remembered the night she and Brandon and her parents had all dined together and ended the evening on the dance floor.

"Then...why did you come back?''

Angie gave her a look of bland surprise as she went back to the table for the other pan. "Because you'd have been left here by yourself with nothing to sell.''

Becky scolded her with a look for evading her and followed her to the oven. "If I'd found my father after a lifetime of thinking he was dead, and my mother—who was the primary reason I'd stuck myself out in the woods in the first place—decided to stay with him, in Beverly Hills, of all places, then I'd have stayed.''

Angie closed the oven door and set the timer. "I thought they needed some time alone together. And that's their life, not mine. I belong in my tearoom kitchen.''

"Was it that gorgeous man who came here with your father?"

Angie ignored the question and went back to the table, detouring by the doors into the tearoom, hoping the bell over the door had failed and a customer had arrived and would require Becky's attention. No such luck.

She grabbed a rag from the sudsy water in the sink and wiped off her worktable.

"A man called while you were on your way in to the shop," Becky said.

Angie's heart shot against her ribs and she stopped scrubbing. Hope fluttered despite her grim acceptance. "Who?" she demanded.

Becky studied her narrowly, noting her reaction. "The paper-products distributor," she replied, admitting with a look that she'd set her up. "So, it *was* the handsome Prinz."

Angie went back to scrubbing, wanting desperately to run and scream and carry on. But your life was your life and you had to live it—however it played out.

"Don't you have something to do?" she asked Becky pointedly.

Becky leaned on her elbows on the other side of the wide table and confronted Angie with a stubborn expression. "Angie, you went away enthused, excited and effervescent. And you came home...plastic. Usually it takes a man to do that amount of damage to a woman's psyche in that small amount of time."

Angie leaned both hands on the table and looked

wearily across it at her friend. "All right, Becky. It was love at first sight for me, and lust at first sight for Brandon. All I want out of life is a happy little family and a tearoom. All he wants out of life is to not be bothered with vows and promises. Now, can we drop it and get on with our work?" She glanced at her watch. "I have to leave for an appointment after the lunch rush, so I have a lot to get done in the meantime."

"I'm sorry," Becky said gravely.

"Yeah," Angie agreed quietly. "Me, too."

Becky gathered up an armful of to-go boxes and went to the swinging doors into the tearoom. She turned before leaving. "You know," she said gently, "I've been married two years now, and I can tell you that men have a 'no' gene in their makeup. They say no to everything when they're first approached because refusing whatever it is keeps them in charge. If they say yes, they're afraid things will move out of their control. Sometimes, though, when they've had a chance to think about it, they change their minds."

Angie smiled at Becky. "I don't care if he changes his mind. Mine is made up." She spread both arms and looked around her kitchen. "This is what I want, and this is what I'm going to have."

Becky pushed her way through the doors and disappeared.

BRANDON DROVE into the town of Gray Goose Lake just after 5:00 p.m. The sidewalks were busy with last-minute shoppers, and the small downtown intersection cluttered with cars as others headed home.

He turned the rental car he'd picked up at the airport onto the side street, parked and made a mental note to remember the speeding ticket he'd stashed in the glove compartment.

He sprinted to the corner, then around it, almost colliding with a woman whose arms were filled with packages. He apologized, then hurried up the street to the Tintagel Tearoom.

He felt as though he would explode if he didn't see Angie's face in the next few minutes. The wait for the afternoon flight, the interminable hour in the air, the commuter flight from Sacramento to Redding, then the drive here had shredded his nerves to rag.

Now that he'd admitted to himself that he did love her, that he *could* love her, he felt free of a lifelong burden. His childhood had been like an anvil on his chest, on his belief in himself and his ability to give with an open heart.

But the evidence of his own face in the photo of Angie and Neil couldn't be denied.

All he had to do was make Angie understand why and how he'd come to his senses.

He burst into the tearoom, the woman at the counter placing an order turning to look at him with obvious disapproval. He recognized the waitress behind the counter as the one who'd cagily refused to give him and Mike Angie's address. Her badge reminded him that her name was Becky.

Over her head was a sign on the wall advertising new additions to the menu. Among them was Bread Pudding with *Crème Anglaise*.

Brandon took that as a good sign that although Angie had run off, she hadn't abandoned everything to do with her week in Beverly Hills.

Becky smiled and looked pleased to see him. "I'll be right with you," she said.

The woman ordering pointed through the glass case at a poppyseed cake. "I'll take that if it's fresh."

"It was made this morning," Becky assured her, reaching in to pull out the plate on which it rested.

"And if the glaze isn't too rich. Is it rich?"

Becky smiled patiently. "No. It's perfect. You bought one last week for your bridge club, remember?"

The woman sighed, fidgeted and studied the case. "Yes, and as I recall I thought it *was* a little rich. Maybe I should rethink this."

Brandon didn't have the patience to wait his turn and spotted the double doors that led into the back. With a wave at Becky, intended to be an apology for his intrusion, he skirted the glass case and went through the doors.

He found a spotless kitchen that seemed to have everything in it a baker could want—but it didn't have what *he* wanted. Angie.

He peered out a back door into a small graveled area where a little white Toyota was parked, but there was no sign of Angie's Volvo.

He pushed his way back into the tearoom, where the customer now wanted a detailed list of ingredients in a marbled pound cake.

"Excuse me a moment," Becky said to the customer, and moved farther along the case and beckoned to Brandon. "Mr. Prinz," she called quietly. "I think Angie went home."

"You're not sure?"

"No. She had an appointment this afternoon that she didn't come back from. She just called to say she'd be in in the morning."

"Who did she have the appointment with?"

"I don't know. She didn't say." Becky frowned worriedly. "But she's edgy and fragile and she sounded like she was crying when she called. I'm worried about her."

Instant anxiety crushed his feelings of freedom and renewal. "Have you called her at home?"

"Her answering machine is picking up calls." Becky glowered at him suddenly from over a lattice-crust apple pie in a domed glass cover. "Maybe I should know why you're here before I tell you where to find her. You're the culprit at the bottom of her miseries."

Guilt doubled his anxiety. He nodded ruefully. "I know I am. But I'm here to fix that."

She studied him consideringly, then gave him a quick smile. "When she's stressed, she turns on the answering machine, locks the door and goes up into this little sitting room she's made in the attic, and listens to George Strait and crochets tea cozies for the shop."

Brandon blew her a kiss as he headed for the door. He ran to the car, raced out to the small acreage with the apple tree and the faded little country cottage. His heart leaped when he saw the Volvo in the driveway.

He went to the door and rang the bell.

ANGIE GROANED over the interruption. She was settled in an old wicker rocker, a towel over her just-washed hair, a skein of forest green worsted in her lap and a Clint Black song about loving and leaving crooning to her from her little boom box. She'd found she couldn't listen to George Strait because his voice revived memories of the drive south with Brandon and Mike.

She ignored the doorbell, knowing Becky was at the shop until six and she'd paid the paperboy last week. She didn't care to talk to anyone else.

She checked the pattern from which she worked, counted the stitches from her last turn and did a triple crochet stitch.

The doorbell rang again.

She concentrated on her stitches.

Then what sounded like an angry fist pounded on the door.

With a few words she'd learned from a hockey player's daughter at boarding school, she dumped the pile of yarn in her lap into the needlework basket beside her chair and pushed herself to her feet.

She turned off the boom box, went to the window and thrust it up. She had to get onto her knees to look out of it.

"What do you want?" she demanded, leaning out to see over the climbing roses.

A figure took several steps backward away from the house to look up at her. It was male and dressed in jeans and a sweater the color of her yarn. Brandon!

Angie's heart punched out at her with a shocked jolt, and she had to hold on to the sill to prevent herself from pitching forward and down three stories into the yard.

"Angie!" he shouted. He was smiling.

She wished for a cauldron of hot oil and repeated her demand. "What do you want?"

"You!" he replied.

"We've had this conversation!" She drew her head back in to pull down the window.

"Wait!" he called: "Will you marry me?"

The words ricocheted around the low-ceilinged little room, hitting walls, floor, window and vibrating in her brain.

She leaned slowly out the window, conducting a personal little war against the "Yes! Yes!" that was trying to force its way from her lips.

"Have you lost your mind?" she asked.

He put both hands over the left side of his chest and smiled up at her. "No. My heart! Can you come down?"

"You told me there was nothing *in* your heart!"

"I was wrong! There's a promise there to love you and be with you always!"

Angie felt that flutter of hope again, like a timid sparrow in her chest. She wanted to believe it, but she found it difficult to trust something he'd been so reluctant to give. He probably just missed having her around to scrub his back and warm his bed. Once he got over that, he would find love too demanding again.

"Well, I'm sorry," she said, her voice strained in a tight throat. "You're too late. You may have come to believe in love, but now I've lost faith in it. Go home, Prinz!"

She leaned back into the room again and prepared to close the window.

"Hey!" he shouted, apparently undaunted by her refusal. "If you won't come down, will you lower your hair so I can climb up?"

With a grim smile for the fairy tale that had been the catalyst for this mercurial interruption in her life, she leaned out the window again and yanked the towel off her head, revealing the pixie cut she'd gotten early that afternoon. It wasn't an inch long anywhere on her head, and though the hairdresser at Ginger's two-chair salon swore that it was chic and feminine, Angie knew the moment she'd done it that it had been a terrible mistake. She'd done it out of pique and acute depression, and the need to erase from her memory images of Brandon's hands in it.

She saw his look of openmouthed surprise, heard a gasp, as though of pain.

"Can't do that, handsome Prinz!" she shouted back at him, tears springing to her eyes, clogging her throat. "I don't have what you need any longer! Now, go away!"

Angie slammed the window down and fell back onto her sweat-bottomed backside and sobbed. Oh, fine! Now he comes for her. Now, when she'd turned off her feelings, thrown away all her dreams, stuffed herself painfully back into the old life that had seemed fine just a week ago but was mournfully empty now. Having spent a week with her father in a sun-drenched old house in Beverly Hills, with Dunston who cooked like a dream and was wonderful company, meeting Emilio and Robin Atkins and Jack Hammond and Neil

Delaney, who'd all but disproven the notion that Southern California people were frivolous and vain, made her feel suddenly out of place here.

She wouldn't let herself think about how the past thirty-six hours without Brandon had made the simple instinct of putting one foot in front of the other seem like such an effort. Absence from him was like subtle torture—it wouldn't kill her, but it would never stop hurting.

"Angie!" she heard him shout.

She covered her ears, refusing to succumb to the emotional burst of knowing he'd probably flown out here to bring her back—that he'd proposed marriage. Because as hard as it had been for him to come to those terms, she couldn't trust them to be permanent.

"Angie!"

She pressed her hands more tightly against her ears, wondering why she could still hear him through a closed window. He was three stories down.

No. She wasn't falling for it. He could stay in the yard shouting for her until midnight and she wasn't coming down. He'd rejected her and while he was completely within his rights to do so, he wasn't going to get the opportunity to do it a second time.

"Angie!" She dropped her hands from her ears, thinking in confusion that he'd sounded closer that time. Had that been her imagination?

"Angie, I'm coming up!"

What? How? She opened the window and looked down, to find him climbing the trellis on which the wild roses clung.

He muttered an epithet and freed one hand from the

trellis to shake it in pain. He looked up at her. He had almost reached the second floor. Her bedroom window was within reach.

"Angie, give me a break," he pleaded. "Come and open this window!"

"Get down this instant!" she shouted at him. "What do you think you're doing?"

"Are you coming down?"

He put his hand on the trellis again and resumed his climb. "Then I'm coming up."

"I don't want to see you!"

"Too bad. I have to see you."

"You're going to fall off that trellis!"

"Then open the window for me! Come on, Angie! This is as high as the trellis goes. Open the window or I'll break it!"

Angry with him for not retreating, she slammed the attic window closed again in wordless defiance of his request.

She sat on the floor, her arms folded on her knees, and listened to the scraping sound of his shoes against the siding.

Who did he think he was? The prince from *Rapunzel* who could scale the tower wall?

"Angie, the trellis is going to give!"

Angie heard the creak of old wood and remembered with sudden horror that in the fairy tale, the prince jumped from the tower when confronted by the witch who had removed Rapunzel, and though he'd survived, he'd been blinded by the thornbushes.

The holly bush under her bedroom window would certainly do Brandon no good.

With a few more swear words and a heart aching with confusion and the pressure of holding on to long-spent anger, she raced down the attic stairs, tripping and catching herself, then running down the rest of them and around the corner into her room.

She scrambled over the bed to reach the window and push it up.

Brandon held on to the trellis and hooked a leg over the windowsill.

Angie look down at the trellis and saw that it appeared perfectly sound.

"I thought you said it was breaking," she accused.

Brandon, now standing beside her on the blue bedroom carpet, brushed himself off and grinned. He was wearing the jacket she'd bought him at Disneyland. Vivid memories of that wonderful day and evening assaulted her.

"I said it was *going* to give," he corrected. "And I'm sure it would have if I'd had to wait much longer." He shook his head at her and scolded mildly, "You heartless wench. You'd have let me fall to my death."

She walked around the bed away from him. "It's only two stories. You'd only have fallen to your fracture."

"Angie." He stopped her at the foot of the bed and turned her around. His dark eyes were serious suddenly, and he gathered her into the loose circle of his arms. "I'm sorry it's taken me so long to see the truth. I truly didn't think I had love in me."

The flutter of hope inside her now had the wing beat

of a condor. She kept her arms folded over it. "What makes you think you do now?"

"I have this photograph in the car," he said with an enigmatic smile, "which I'll show you later. But I discovered on the way here that it's more than that. I thought nothing could grow in me where other people planted love. I guess..." He shook his head, apparently mystified by something. "I thought feeling love was something you did yourself. But now I understand that the love in me is the love *you* put there, so as long as you love me, I'll always feel it. And the love *you* feel—" he tapped an index finger gently over her heart "—*I* put there. So, see? I can do it."

Angie put her right hand over her heart where he'd touched, everything inside her softening, melting, warming. "I need that there, Brandon. You're sure you won't get tired of keeping it there?"

"Isn't it there now?" he asked.

It was. Even under the anguish and anger and disappointment of the past thirty-six hours, it remained. "Yes," she whispered.

He smiled and leaned down to kiss her lightly on the mouth, looking triumphant. "And that was from over five hundred miles away. Imagine what I can do with you beside me."

He thought he would die of relief when she threw her arms around him and sobbed and laughed against his throat.

He rested his chin on her hair and felt the prickly dampness of it against him. The utter grief he'd felt earlier when she'd ripped the towel off to reveal her